Old & New Tales to Read in a Hammock

(Both anthologies updated now in one book
with some new stories to enjoy!)

Robyn P Murray

PUBLISHERS: Robyn P Murray Hirst

Auckland New Zealand

© Copyright 2016 Robyn P Murray

ISBN: 978-0-9941260-2-3

A catalogue record for this book is available from the
New Zealand National Library Wellington, New Zealand.

Fiction, short stories, family life, relationships

INTRODUCTION

When I published my first collection of short stories TALES TO READ IN A HAMMOCK and later MORE TALES TO READ IN A HAMMOCK., I received some lovely feedback and was constantly asked 'When is the next book available?'

They quickly sold out and I decided instead of reprinting both books again, to combine them and add a few more tantalising tales for readers to enjoy.

I hope you find TALES OLD & NEW TO READ IN A HAMMOCK as enjoyable as the others. There is humour, pathos, romance, murder and the unexpected that life can throw up from time to time.

I love to hear from readers who buy my children's books, short stories (and soon a novel) and receive their comments. If you would like to contact me at robmur@xtra.co.nz or http://robynpmurray.com/ I'd be very happy to hear from you.

Dedicated to family and friends who love reading
Particularly the younger generation all of
whom encourage me to keep writing.

Robyn P Murray has also published children's illustrated
books

- ROGER THE ROOSTER OF AMBURY PARK FARM
- EL GALLO ROGELIO DE LA GRANJA PARK FARM
  (Spanish translation of Roger the Rooster)
- THE SPIRIT OF CAMERON OF AMBURY PARK
  FARM.
- JACK'S MOUNTAINS
- NEAL WILLIAM'S ADVENTURE
- THE LAZY GLAMEROUS GODMOTHER
- Contributed to THE BEST OF TWISTY CHRISTMAS
  TALES for 7 – 12 year old children.

Short Story Anthologies for general reading by all ages:
- TALES TO READ IN A HAMMOCK
- MORE TALES TO READ IN A HAMMOCK

- Contributed to and published in conjunction with
  Kerrie Anne Spicer a collection of poetry, fiction
  and more writings of the Mangere Bridge Writers
  Group. VIEWS FROM THE BRIDGE.

CONTENTS

INTRODUCTION iii

LEAVING DANNY 1

NATURE'S ARTIST 8

THE GIRL WHO WAS FOUND IN A

SEAGULL'S NEST 15

WHERE DID YOU GET THOSE EYES? 26

PAROS 39

THE WELL TRAVELLED SUITCASE 46

MORNING ROUNDS – MRS JONES 54

BANANA SPLIT 58

THE TWIG 64

THE UNFINISHED DANCE 74

HOT FEET 99

WEEKEND IN RUSSELL 107

FINDING MAUREEN 135

THERE'S A COFFIN IN THE LOUNGE 146

A BODY IN THE WOODS 157

A NEW YORK CHRISTMAS 161

SOUNDS 167

THE CURIOUS CASE OF THE 170

POISIONOUS POT PLANT 170

CUTHBERT AND THE 176

THESPIANS 176

A CUP OF TEA GRAN? 181

A BUG - NOT IN A RUG 186

LETTER TO MY SOULMATE 190

ESCAPE FROM MARRAKESH   195
THE STALKER   225
SPEED BUMP   231
ERNEST AND HENRY   238
SEE YOU IN PARIS   245
THE CAT CAME BACK   250
A FEW DAYS IN COURT   256
THE PRAYER   262
THE WATCHER BEING WATCHED   265
WHAT IF?   270
EDIE AND JOSIE   282
POOR DEVIL   295
MARY'S CHRISTMAS MIRACLE   303
HOME FROM HOME   319
FRIENDS, MEMORIES & A LEGACY   321
ABOUT THE AUTHOR   330

LEAVING DANNY

It was ten past six on a cold wet winter evening when Maureen left Danny. She remembered the time particularly as she was strap-hanging on the bus going home after work. Her eyes were level with the watch of a tall young man whose hand was above hers, holding onto the pole midway along the bus.

Suddenly the bus driver slammed on the brakes; a cyclist weaving through the traffic had cut across his path. Everyone standing lurched forward and the bags of groceries for dinner Maureen was clutching that she had rushed to pick up during her lunch hour fell on the floor of the bus and disappeared under seats. It was the proverbial straw that broke her stoic reserve of keeping on coping.

1

"Stop the bus," she yelled. Pushing her way to the door she clambered off leaving bags of fruit, vegetables and chicken where they were. All the passengers stared, some with sympathy, some disapprovingly.

Maureen gazed at the bus as it disappeared in the rain and traffic. "I can't cope," she muttered. "I can't do this anymore."

She was standing outside a small pub, where lights spilt onto the wet pavement invitingly. Pushing her way through the door, the room felt warm and cozy with a fire burning and the quiet murmur of people relaxing at the end of their working day. Walking over to the fireplace, she sat down on an old settle and stretched her sodden feet to the fire.

"Like a drink love?" said a young waitress, who was clearing glasses and wiping tables.

"Mmm! Yes please, I'll have an Irish Coffee hot and strong," replied Maureen.

"Coming up, anything to eat, garlic bread nibbles?" said the waitress cheerily.

"Thanks, whatever's handy."

Her mind was still a blank. Maureen had got into the habit of pushing her thoughts away, coping with whatever had to be done in the next hour or day for Danny and the children. Only when she was at work in the City Planning Department did she feel she was part of the real world.

The young waitress put a steaming mug of Irish Coffee and a platter of bread, dips and cheese in front of her with a smile. "There you are love, that should warm you up."

"Thank you," said Maureen gratefully. She felt the warming coffee slip down her throat and her feet coming back to life. Somehow she felt different, better than she had felt for a very long time. Although her hair was dripping down her neck and wet clothes sticking to her body, for some reason she wasn't stressing that she wouldn't be home in time to prepare dinner.

For Danny who would be sitting reading the paper, Vanessa slouched in front of television chewing her hair and endlessly texting her friends; Bryan hypnotized in front of his x-box games. None of them would have thought to start preparing dinner or put washing on. Their coats and bags would be lying in the hall where they'd dropped them. Just sitting, waiting for Maureen to call them for dinner when it was ready.

A sudden thought entered Maureen's head – I've left Danny. She paused wondering where that thought came from; then realized that was what she had done. She didn't feel guilty, just detached. Relief and a little fear rushed through her body as she thought back over the last 17 years. How had she become more and more cowed and browbeaten, her confidence gone?

Life was – nothing – she was living in a vacuum at the beck and call of her demanding family. How had she become such a victim?

The evening went on and in the home that Maureen had created for them, three people sitting, waiting, suddenly realized that something was different. There was no smell of dinner being prepared, no noise from the kitchen. The lights hadn't been switched on and they were as usual waiting to be called for dinner while watching whatever was showing on TV.

"Hey where's Mum?" said Bryan, "I'm hungry and I need my kit to go out to karate."

"I didn't hear her come in," said Vanessa, "and I need my costume for the dress rehearsal of the play tonight."

Danny looked up. "Well why aren't you getting your gear ready?" he said crossly. He had a moment of frisson wondering where Maureen was then snarled, "she is probably helping them out in that stupid office, very inconsiderate, I'm going out myself later."

"But she would have phoned," said Vanessa. They all looked at each other with a faint feeling of unease. But nobody phoned the office to check if she had left for the evening and no one moved to organize something to eat or sort out their kit.

A little later a taxi drove up. Maureen turned the key in the lock and strode confidently inside. Three accusing faces glared at her.

"We haven't had our dinner, we need our costume/kit," said the kids in unison.

"It's not good enough Maureen; I'm supposed to be meeting other managers from out of town to discuss strategy for next quarter."

"Oh dear!" said Maureen, "Don't you mean you are going down the pub Danny? There is plenty of bread in the freezer and eggs on the bench top; you could have made something for yourselves. Bryan and Vanessa did you get your gear for me to sort out at the weekend? Of course not, as usual you leave everything for me to organize at the last minute. It is not my fault if they are not ready."

Three sets of jaws dropped.

Hanging her coat up Maureen picked up her bag and climbed the stairs saying over her shoulder, "I've eaten, I'm going upstairs to have a long hot soak in the bath, then I will hop into bed. In the spare room, Danny. I am going to read my library book and I know how annoyed you get when the light is on."

For once the whining stopped. Shocked, nobody could think of anything to say.

Turning at the top of the stairs, Maureen said firmly, "Breakfast will be on the table at nine o'clock tomorrow. It's Saturday morning so you don't have to rush off, no school or going to work. I want to let you know about some decisions I've made. Life as we know it is about to change – don't be late!" Without waiting for a reply she turned and closed the bathroom door firmly behind her.

Danny, Vanessa and Bryan stood at the bottom of the stairs in disbelief trying to take in what Maureen had said, then they heard the sound of bath water running, the smell of bath salts drifting out and the unusual sound of – singing.

Later, snuggled down in the spare room with a tray of tea on the bedside table, Wilbur the old cat tucked purring under her arm, hot water bottles at her back and feet and library book at hand, Maureen thought over the events of the past few hours and how it seemed her life had changed forever. She wasn't quite sure what she was going to say to her family tomorrow at breakfast but knew with certainty that her life was changing for the better, and she hoped eventually her family would come to feel the same.

That silly sod on the bicycle will never know how he saved my life by almost causing an accident when he cut in front of the bus. She grinned to herself, snuggled down, picked up her book and began to read.

The Beginning.

First published in Her Business & Lifestyle Magazine and read on Writers on Air.

NATURE'S ARTIST

Two figures stood motionless on the deck of the holiday home where they were staying, watching for the familiar pre-dawn view of the beach at the bottom of the hill. It was the first day of the New Year and two old friends were enjoying a favourite place and time of day for their holiday together.

They tried to manage their busy lives and spend their holiday together every year but as time went on and they both became more successful in their careers and lives, another year often slipped by before they knew it.

This year by chance or good luck they were both in New Zealand at the same time.

The rising sun shot fingers of gold along the beach illuminating water and sand. Suddenly as though an artist had dipped his brush in rose pink and drawn it along the white foam, the edges of the crashing surf were no longer white but a delicate pink. As the sun climbed higher from behind the hills the beach was filled with a glorious light. It highlighted White Island out in the bay with the usual puff of smoke rising in the air. A distant ship on the horizon and several fishing boats heading for their favourite places to let down their nets completed the scene.

"A photographer is never around when a picture like that unfolds." Joe smiled at Marnie and they sat at the table on the deck to breakfast on fruit, bread warm from the oven, and coffee.

Marnie and Joe had met as students when they enrolled in a Media Studies course in Christchurch almost 25 years ago. They found in each other a soul mate, both determined to succeed, encouraging each other when their tutors urged them to make more effort. They were ambitious and each had a passionate determination to succeed and make a difference. They both worked hard and strove to be the best in their group.

After graduating Joe left to take up a scholarship in London before being offered a prime opportunity with Reuters News Agency in Germany. Marnie's tutor, recognizing her talent, suggested she freelance for newspapers in Australia and New Zealand. When she had really learned her craft she was commissioned to offer opinion and insight for media around the globe,

Working hard over the years, gaining experience and knowledge, they both earned highly respected awards and comments from their peers.

They kept in touch, met when their busy schedules allowed, but somehow they were never in the same place long enough to take their relationship to the next level. In the end they both made a pact to meet annually, either the last week of year or the first week of the New Year. They had a favourite spot in New Zealand in the Bay of Plenty, where they had spent many University vacations swimming, talking, planning how they were going to bring integrity back into journalism and make a difference by reporting the truth. They drank cheap red wine from a local vineyard, cooked fish they caught and made love under the stars.

"You know Marnie," said Joe, "I travel all over the world, stay at the best hotels at times, but no one makes the first cup of coffee for me like you."

"Just the right amount of coffee in the machine, brewed for the right amount of time, a dash of milk, 1/3rd of a teaspoon of Manuka honey, to sweeten slightly; not a ½ not a ¼ of a teaspoon but a 1/3rd. Perfect."

They both laughed at memories of other mornings and shared coffee. "Not that I have been making many coffees for you in recent times," said Marnie wryly.

"I know," said Joe, "the last few years have been so hectic and this one even more so." He rubbed a hand over his face as if to wipe out the catastrophic events all over the world that he had recently reported on. Haiti, China, weather chaos in the USA and Europe. Uprisings in the Middle East. Miners trapped with the world holding its breath waiting for rescue, with unbelievably positive results in Chile; then ending the year reporting on the tragic fatal explosions in Pike River Mine in the South Island of New Zealand.

The adrenaline which drove him to follow another unfolding news story was loosening its grip. After years of catching the first flight to whereever in the world the latest drama was unfolding; the ground imploding, another disaster to be reported, uprisings, suicide bombers, all needing him to bring breaking news to the world.

Often Joe was the first correspondent on the scene and his measured tones reporting calmly were respected and valued around the world.

He no longer found his job challenging. The image of another disaster, yet another war, suffering of innocent people, invaded his dreams and disturbed his sleep.

"Marnie I am losing heart and the stomach for this kind of life," sighed Joe. "I can't switch off any more. The innate cruelty that people can inflict on one another, the horror of loss and death. I long to denounce the Generals, the incompetence of Government Officials who prevent aid reaching areas of natural disasters. When I learn of the greed of smooth business operators taking advantage of trusting people conning them out of their hard earned savings, being impartial is becoming more difficult. And I'm tired. I think it is time I hung up my Foreign Correspondent's hat."

Marnie poured more coffee and said, "What would you like to replace this hectic life you have lived for the past 20 years? Flying off to a different destination every week or so, you might find it hard to be in the same place for long."

"I don't know. I'm tired. It may be an idea to take a sabbatical for a year, think about the next stage of my life. Maybe I'll write a book or just write the memories for myself; it might exorcise the images behind my eyes." Joe sighed, breathed deeply and closed his eyes, turning his face to the sun now shining on the deck.

Over the years they both had relationships; made plans for a life with other people. They both broke their engagements off before the weddings took place. Somehow they couldn't make that final commitment. A week before Joe's marriage in New York to Rochelle he found himself thinking more and more of Marnie and the times they spent together, relaxed, talking into the night laughing over silly things. He was relieved when another crisis blew up in the Middle East and he flew out cancelling the wedding.

Marnie had lived with Thomas in Sydney for two years. They bought a tiny house on the North Shore near the water, and were fairly happy. As time went on Thomas wanted Marnie to give up her 'little' job and help him build his business, i.e. do all his paper work and accounts. The third business venture since she had known him. Eventually she realized that she could no longer bale Thomas out after he became bored with the routine of running a business and the hard slog needed to build it up. She saw his charm but finally walked away and was still waiting to be paid out her share of the house. Although they had both signed the mortgage, she had paid for everything. She cut her losses and flew back to New Zealand.

Joe sat up and looked at the familiar figure beside him with her green eyes, and pageboy dark hair. There was a distinctive lock of hair which had turned white overnight before final exams.

"Oh! Marnie I take you for granted, you've been in my life for the past twenty odd years. I come and go and you never protest when I disappear for months or even years. I turn up and you smile and I immediately feel better." Leaning over he tucked the silver lock of hair behind her ear, kissed her waiting mouth and murmured, "What would I do without you?"

Smiling at each other they knew that at last this was their time and they would spend the rest of their lives together.

THE END

THE GIRL WHO WAS FOUND
IN A SEAGULL'S NEST

Christmas Eve and the O'Neill family had come home from the Christmas service in the village, finished dinner, and were settling round the big log fire. It would be the last Christmas together as Dominic and Liam, the two oldest sons, were leaving in the New Year to begin their new lives.

Grace and Dylan O'Neill with their family of six tall strong sons, all with dark hair and blue eyes; Dominic, Liam, Cormac, James and Michael and their seventh child, a red-haired brown-eyed daughter ten years old named Cordelia. The extended O'Neill family had lived in the fishing village for the past 400 years. Over the generations many of their family had emigrated to America, England, Canada or

15

Australia to give their families more opportunities. Dylan and Grace had decided to stay.

They renovated the big old house Dylan's great grandfather had built and settled down to raise their growing family. They had a few animals, grew what vegetables and fruit trees which survived the wild winter storms and Dylan went out with the fishing boat which belonged to several families in the village.

They had a secret that few people knew about and tonight the truth would be revealed and questions answered.

In the New Year Liam was joining his Uncle Daniel's ship to begin five years as an apprentice ship's engineer. Dominic, with the encouragement and support of the local Headmaster, was joining a major newspaper in London as a very junior reporter. Both had an opportunity to build good careers although they were sad at leaving the village they had grown up in, their Mam and Dad, brothers and little sister where they had been so happy. Young men almost, they were excited at the prospect of a new life in front of them.

After much laughter and reminiscences, everyone grew quiet thinking of growing up on the big house on the cliff and their happy childhood. Helping their father with the animals on the land and learning to fish on the village fishing boat. All of them growing up with a love of books and learning encouraged by their Mam, Dad and the school master in the local school.

Then Cordelia's quiet little voice broke the silence. "Dad, where did I come from?"

"Why, Cordelia, we've always told you, we found you in a Seagull's Nest. He laughed and the boys laughed too. The very idea – in a Seagull's Nest!

Then Mam said, "I think the time is right now Dylan, Cordelia has a right to know the truth and she is old enough to understand."

"Are you sure now Grace," replied Dylan with a concerned look on his face.

"Yes I'm sure, this is the right time," said Mam.

The boys straightened up, no more slouching or lying on the floor. This sounded serious.

Cordelia said, "What do you mean the truth?"

"Hush now pet, Daddy will tell you everything, come and sit by my knee." Grace put her arm out and drew Cordelia close where she

17

rested on her Mam's knee. She snuggled in and looked hard at her Dad.

"It all began the night of the hundred year storm," said Dad.

"I remember that night," said Dominic, "the big hawthorne tree was split in two by a lightning strike."

Liam and Sam remembered how the wind had howled round the house and they were afraid the roof was going to come off.

Then came the eerie ghostly sound of the lifeboat siren howling through the storm, warning the village a boat was in trouble. Dylan was one of the volunteers who took the lifeboat out to try and rescue a boat struggling in the mountainous seas and hopefully save lives.

He struggled into his wet weather gear, his big boots that could grip the wet deck, took his torch and Grace gave him a flask of tea.

"May all the Angels and Saints preserve you and bring everyone on the lifeboat and those poor souls lost at sea safely home." She hugged her husband tightly. She and Dominic held the door while Dylan struggled out into the storm.

"Look after your mother and brothers, son," said Dylan to his oldest boy.

"I will Dad," Dominic promised.

It was a hard struggle to get down to the port where the other volunteers had made their way. John the Skipper gave them their orders and taking up their positions they launched the lifeboat into the treacherous stormy sea.

"The distress flares came from beyond the lighthouse. We must make our way there. Hold on tight and keep a sharp look out," shouted John above the noise of the wind and crashing sea.

The boat seemed at times to stand straight upright as it rode the mountainous waves, others it was a miracle it didn't turn over.

For hours they battled up and down by the rocks under the lighthouse but could not see any sign of a boat or survivors. Finally and reluctantly John gave the order to turn for home.

Dylan was in the prow tied firmly with rope so he wouldn't be washed overboard. As the lifeboat turned for home he spotted an upturned life raft from a boat which must have sunk. They continued to search and search but there was no sign of life. Reluctantly they turned for home, pulled their lifeboat up to the boat shed and John said, "We'll clean up in the morning lads, go home and get dried out. We search the shoreline in the morning for any signs of wreckage or bodies."

Wearily the men turned for home.

Dylan took the cliff path home. He usually didn't come this way but hoped it would be quicker. Almost at the top of the climb he stumbled as part of the path had given way and he tumbled down the steep cliff, stopped by a sturdy gorse bush clinging to the cliff face.

Suddenly there was silence. The wind dropped and he heard a faint mewling sound coming from where the seagulls built their nests. Thinking it might be a small animal in trouble; he rubbed the rain water from his eyes and saw to his astonishment a small cradle fashioned like a little curragh stuck by a rock where an enormous wave must have thrown it up. He blinked again as he thought he saw a small hand come up. He scrambled over, grabbed the tiny cradle and saw a little figure like a doll strapped in. Tucking the cradle under his arm he scrambled somehow up the cliff and ran as fast as he could to home, a warm fire, and Grace. She would look after this little baby.

"So you see Cordelia," said her Dad softly, "when I said we found you in a Seagull's Nest, it was true."

Everyone was quiet, trying to imagine the night Cordelia arrived in their family.

"I gave you your name," Dominic suddenly remembered. "We were reading *The Tempest* at school and Cordelia was in it and her name in Gaelic means Daughter of the Sea".

"That's right," said Dad, "and we also gave her Grace after her new Mammy. You know Cordelia your Mam never slept for 10 days and nights while she nursed you and tried to get you to take some milk, bring your fever down. The doctor and priest didn't think you would survive."

"But you did my darling girl. One night I fell asleep in the rocking chair, I jolted awake and there you were, looking up at me with those big brown eyes, your fever gone and you were safe," said Grace, smiling at the memory of those worrying days.

"But do you mean you are not my real Mam and Dad, my brothers are not my brothers?" Cordelia's lip trembled.

"Now, now my pet," soothed her Mam, "you are truly as much our child as the boys who were born in this house."

"I read a long time ago Cordelia," said Dad, "that children choose the parents and family they are going to live with and as much as the boys chose us, you certainly chose us to be your

21

family. Why do you think I decided to come by the cliff path that night and the storm suddenly was still so I could hear your tiny cry? Oh yes my pet, we are as much your family as the young people who gave you life and we believe perished in the hundred year storm that night. Although we tramped the shoreline for weeks we never found any trace of them."

"The doctor, the priest and I searched for any record of where you came from but there was no trace. In the end the doctor and priest decided it would be best to stay with the loving family who had welcomed you into their home."

"Remember Dylan," laughed Grace, "the night before the storm became so fierce we were talking and laughing about those rambunctious boys of ours and saying what they needed was a civilizing influence of a sister in the house to keep those boyos in check."

"By the next morning we had our wish, a quiet, clever, serene, beautiful daughter to add a calming loving addition to our houseful of boys," said Dylan solemnly.

Cordelia's brothers all came and hugged and kissed their little sister and it seemed they all had bright eyes hearing about the eventful start to her life.

"Liam," said Mam, "run up and fetch the big box at the back of my cupboard."

"Right, but don't tell anything more until I come down." He thundered up the stairs and was back in a moment. He put the large box down by Mam's chair.

"Open the box darlin'," smiled Mam to Cordelia.

She turned the lock and looked inside. Wrapped in a soft blanket was the tiny cradle shaped like a curragh.

"Oh!" breathed Cordelia, "it is so small."

"To think it survived, and you too, the hundred-year storm. It goes to show you were meant to land on the cliff by the seagull's nest, I was meant to climb up the cliff path and the storm was meant to drop so I could hear your little cry," said Dad with tears in his eyes.

Cordelia went over and tightly hugged her dear Dad, then her Mam and all her brothers crowded round and hugged her so tightly she knew she was the luckiest girl in the world to be surrounded by all this love and affection.

That night Cordelia had the dream which had appeared from time to time. A young couple, the man with red gold hair like hers, the woman with brown hair and brown eyes, smiling at her. This time she heard a voice.

"Cordelia our darling girl, you did indeed choose your family well, we are always watching over you and love you." The dream faded and she never had the dream again.

Cordelia got up and wrapped the quilt that Mam had made around her. She sat down at the desk that Liam and Sam had made for her as a Christmas gift. She began to write an account of all she had heard that night. The curtains of her window were pulled back. As she looked out over the garden at the benches made by her Dad and brothers from the old hawthorne tree; she smiled remembering how they had all carved their names into the wood.

Over the wall the bright moonlight lit up the cliff path covered in snow which had begun to fall as they walked home from church. Suddenly a seagull flew up, disturbed by a predator prowling. The bird flew across the face of the full moon creating an image that Cordelia carried with her for the rest of her life.

THE END

This story began when I remembered a conversation with my Mam as a 3 year old in Ireland. "Where did I come from Mammy?" I asked.
"Why we found you in a seagull's nest" was the reply.
What a great title for a story I thought, a few years back.
Thanks Mam.

WHERE DID YOU GET THOSE EYES?

A few days after the funeral Beth let herself into the apartment and felt her beloved Grandma's calm serene presence so strongly, tears fell unbidden down her face. She couldn't believe that she would never talk, laugh and spend time with her again.

She had promised her mother that she would go through her Grandma's papers and sort out favourite paintings and treasures for family to choose before the apartment went on the market.

After making a coffee Beth sat at the beautiful old desk where her Grandma had loved to sit and write, and looked again at photos of her Mum, Aunt, Uncle, cousins, and family holidays with all of them together. Tucked behind an old fashioned ink pot was a small silver framed photograph of a tall distinguished looking man, smiling at whoever was taking the photograph.

Suddenly Beth jumped up, knocking over her coffee. Fortunately it was almost finished and didn't spill on anything important. She recognized the man in the photograph, or thought she did. She stood up and prowled around. Who was it? Where had she seen him before?

Suddenly she remembered. A man who looked just like the figure in the picture was at Grandma's funeral standing at the back of the church. As she and her family were walking down the aisle, he stood back and as she caught his eye he bowed slightly. His eyes were the most amazing colour. Grey green against a tanned skin. She had felt a shiver run down her spine then she'd carried on out into the sunlight and round to the graveyard for the burial.

In the apartment Beth hurried over to the desk and picked up the photo. It couldn't be the man at the church - it must have been his father or uncle. Who were they? How did Grandma know them? I wonder if Mum knows.

Some hours later Beth had sorted out papers into piles for her Mum and Aunt to see to, threw out old papers that were not of interest, and emptied the drawers. At the back of the bottom drawer was a leather bound book filled with her Grandma's beautiful writing.

Making a fresh pot of coffee Beth sat down and began to read.

When I first arrived in India I travelled slowly, stopping at places Michael and I had planned to visit. We had spent time in the library and travel agents making notes for our planned trip. Ranthambore National Park, located in the Sawai Madhopur district of South Eastern Rajasthan was where I planned to spend the last two weeks of my holiday, relaxing in a beautiful old fashioned comfortable hotel and exploring the nearby National Park.

I was thoroughly enjoying my time travelling alone although it would have been wonderful if Michael had been with me. I had arrived almost two weeks earlier and was beginning to relax. When Michael died so suddenly last year it took time for the girls and me to accept he was gone and move on with our lives.

Beth realized this must have been an account of Grandma's trip made before her Mum married and she was born. Fascinated she turned again to the book.

Michael and I married young just out of University and because I became pregnant so soon with Deidre and a year later with Faith; our planned trip round the world didn't eventuate. Not that we regretted having the girls so quickly - we loved being a family and watching them grow. Deidre was the image of her Dad with his dark hair and blue eyes and Faith like me with red hair and brown eyes. We worked hard and built a good and happy life for our family. We planned when the girls were older and making their way in the world, we would take that long overdue trip round the world.

Both girls were established in University and we were planning a trip to India. We were going to book when Michael returned from a seminar he was attending in Glasgow. He never reached home. A pile up on the motorway on a wet and rainy day left him dead and turned our lives upside down.

Beth reached for a tissue only imagining how her Mum, Grandma and Aunt coped with losing their Dad and husband.

A year after Michael died I decided to take the trip we had planned. The girls were concerned about me going alone but I reassured them it was all well planned.

Peace, tranquility and calm took over my all my senses as I enjoyed the comfort and pleasant fellow travelers at the hotel. Visiting the National Park close by the hotel I marveled at the diverse flora and fauna and felt they were the true treasures of India.

One week after arriving at the hotel I was enjoying a pre-dinner drink on the wide veranda and chatting with other guests when a sudden excruciating pain struck me in the chest and I fell to the ground.

Next I was recovering consciousness drifting in and out of awareness in a hospital bed, connected to machines measuring my vital signs, wearing an oxygen mask and surrounded by medical staff. I could see a tall figure rapidly asking questions of the team around him and checking a chart. He leaned over me and spoke softly. "I'm Charles Grey the heart specialist, do you still have pain?"

He removed the oxygen mask and told me to breathe slowly and asked if I had ever had pain like this previously.

"No never, I've never felt pain like this in my life; I thought I was going to die," I said.

"You could have, if the hotel staff hadn't acted swiftly. I think you have contracted a heart virus," replied Professor Grey.

Charles later told me what happened next. He turned, gave instructions to his team and then as a tranquilizer was being given he felt my hand on his sleeve. He leaned down.

He heard a whisper, "where did you get those eyes?" They were pale grey green, startling in his dark face.

He leaned close to her ear, "from my mother." He smiled.

I murmured, "She must be very beautiful." I didn't hear his soft reply, "she was."

Then I went into cardiac arrest.

I was told it was three days later that I became aware of a dim room and the quiet murmur of voices around me.

Someone said, "She is very lucky to be alive, I can't believe she survived."

"I've never seen the Professor work so long on a patient, he usually accepts when it is too late, but really, I believe he brought her back from the dead," said another voice.

"Oh! Look sleeping beauty is stirring. How you feel Geraldine?" asked the Ward Sister.

"A bit dopey, but what on earth happened? Last thing I remember, besides bits of being in hospital, is enjoying a quiet drink on the verandah of the hotel, then I felt this horrendous pain."

"Professor Grey has been to check on you, he is very pleased with your progress. He is at a fund raising dinner tonight but will call in on his way home, and if you are still awake he will explain everything. Now try and rest, your results are looking good," answered the Sister.

I stretched my limbs checking for any discomfort, nothing, no pain in my chest so I dozed, thanking God that I was alive.

Later that night, the ward was quiet with dimmed lights, and I could see the Ward Sister sitting at her desk talking quietly to the nurses who came and went. A figure appeared at the door of my room and came over to my bed. His shirt was startlingly white in the dim light and an untied bow tie dangled from his collar.

"Ah, I see you have rejoined us in the land of the living." Charles Grey sat on the side of my bed and took my hand. My pulse unaccountably began to race.

"How are you feeling?" he said.

"What happened?" I asked. "I never had heart problems before."

"It looks like a virus which caused inflammation and then a heart attack. It was one of the most unusual I have seen, very interesting from a clinical point of view." He raised his eyebrows and smiled.

I took his hand, tears rolling down my face. "I don't know how to thank you, and you saved my life."

Professor Grey gently brushed my tears away. "Well I think I had to save you, there are many other things for you to achieve in life, besides no one else has complimented me on my eyes as they were dying. When we tried everything else I held your heart in my hands and willed it to start beating again." He smiled. "It worked!"

For several hours we sat and talked about our lives. He had two almost grown sons, and a socialite wife who spent most of her time in Europe attending fashionable parties. Occasionally she flitted home, unsettling everyone and then flying back to the next party on a yacht.

He talked about his work and determination to improve health care for heart patients. About his mother part French, part English who died young with a heart attack when he was 12 because there were no facilities to save her. He went to live with his grandparents, an irascible old retired British Army Colonel and his beautiful Indian wife. Charles's father had died before he was born, climbing in the Swiss Alps. He and his mother Celine had met while students in the Sorbonne.

I told him of my life with Michael and our daughters. How he died last year just as we were planning this trip. I talked of Deidre and Faith's ambitions for the future and my job helping young impoverished mothers to care first for themselves and then their families. About my love of painting and rare and beautiful plants.

We each tried to convey to each other a lifetime of living before fate brought us together.

The next day the Ward Sister told me she had come into the room and stopped. There seemed to be something extraordinary between the two people and in the quiet murmur of their voices which didn't bear interrupting. She quietly turned and left.

The doctor and his patient, who had met only three days earlier and spoken for a few hours, knew there was a connection between them that would never be broken. They also knew they would never meet again.

Reluctantly he finally said, "You must get some rest. I have contacted the Heart Specialist in your home town and the airline you are travelling with. You will be well enough to travel in a few days and will be well cared for on the journey home. Contact David Nicholson at this hospital on your return, I have sent him all my notes and he will keep an eye on you. We studied together and he is a good man. Unfortunately I am flying to Geneva tomorrow morning; I must go as I am the principal speaker, so I shan't see you again.

He paused. "You and my mother are the only women in my life who have touched my heart, and I shall carry yours with me always."

Impulsively I said "Wait, just a moment." I took out my small camera. "I want to remember always this time of my life."

Charles picked up my left hand, turned it over and kissed the palm. I took the photograph.

"Safe journey," he said. Then turned and walked out of the room and my life.

"And to you," I whispered, "for all of your life, safe journey."

There were no more entries in the journal.

Beth sat with tears running down her face. Then she suddenly remembered when Grandma was dying and we were all sitting with her how she had suddenly opened her eyes, looked over my shoulder at the door and said clearly, "where did you get those eyes?" She had smiled, closed her eyes, and drifted away. Now Beth understood her Grandma last words.

She didn't know but at the same time her grandmother was dying thousands of miles away, an eminent heart surgeon was also leaving the world, his sons and grandsons by his bed. Early one morning he opened his eyes, smiled as if he recognized someone, and said clearly, "safe journey." Then closed his eyes and was gone.

She looked again at the little photo and could see the smiling man had been holding the photographer's hand, her Grandma's.

Beth decided to call her Mum. She couldn't wait to tell her about what she had found. As she picked up the phone, the intercom buzzed. "That must be Mum now," she said and buzzed the door release. She went and opened a bottle of wine. We'll need it when I tell her what I discovered.

A knock sounded at the door, she opened it smiling and said, "I unlocked it for you Mum." She staggered back. Standing on the doorstep was the man in the photograph. No, it couldn't be - he was too young.

"Who, who are you? What do you want? Sorry, sorry I've just had a shock."

He put a hand out to steady her.

"I apologize for the intrusion, my name is Charles Grey."

"Did I see you at my Grandma's funeral?" Beth interrupted him.

"Yes you did, you see my Grandfather died recently and I believe he knew or was in love with your Grandmother. I found a diary he wrote and I felt impelled to find the woman he thought about every day since he met her, only to find when I arrived in England that she had died the same day he did."

Beth opened the door wider and invited in the grandson of the man who not only saved her Grandma's life but captured her heart as well. It was extraordinary, unbelievable that such love could endure.

He stretched out his hand and as they clasped hands both felt a jolt of recognition. Maybe fate had decided they were going to have the relationship that their grandparents were denied.

THE END

PAROS

1st September 1975

Dear Charles

I will arrive at the train station 6.15 tomorrow evening. Don't worry about meeting me, I will take a taxi.

I have contacted Croeso Boutique Hotel on the Greek Island of Paros where in the past I have spent several restoring visits. Stephan and Ana have accommodation available for you and will collect you from the ferry when it arrives on Thursday. The air travel is booked with an open ticket and a car will meet you at the airport to take you to the ferry. There will be plenty of time to catch it just in case there are delays with the flight.

Charles, I believe this is an opportunity for you to get away to try and recover from the tragic events of the last year. I am still trying to get my head around it myself and can only imagine how it has affected you.

I will pack your bags. You know how I love packing and organizing people. I'll drive you to the airport Wednesday morning then arrange with Mrs. Banks next door to keep an eye on things while you are away.

I am not giving you the chance to refuse that is why I am 'railroading' you. I know it will take more than a holiday to erase from your mind what has happened but I know that the Island of Paros will bring some peace to your soul.

With fond love
Lavinia.

21st September 1975
Dear Lavinia
Thank you for arranging my stay here on the beautiful Greek Island of Paros. The Croeso Boutique Hotel is everything you promised. This evening I am sitting on the terrace with a chilled bottle of wine, dishes of olives, cheese and bread, breathing the wonderful air and absorbing the light, smell of lemon, wild thyme and pine. A

blazing sun setting below the horizon has turned the Aegean Sea scarlet and gold; and somehow I feel protected, safe, my head not turning over the accident which robbed me of my family and almost my sanity. At times it feels the accident happened only yesterday but I know that it was almost six months ago since that bleak chance of fate of being in the wrong place at the wrong time.

You know the couple who run the Hotel came originally from Wales over 20 years ago, renovated an old farm house. It began as a bed and breakfast but within a few years they never had to advertise as word of mouth meant they were always full. A few years later they extended to the lovely place it is today. Did you know that the name of the hotel Croeso is Welsh for Welcome?

My nervous system is slowly unclenching, and I am seduced by the location, the calm acceptance of my hosts, that I am here to renew my spirit and do not always want to engage in conversation. Other guests are an interesting mixture of people from around the world. One elderly lady from Yorkshire has spent three months of the year here for the last seven years.

At dinner, a few nights ago, we were the only guests staying in and she quietly asked if I minded us having dinner together. How could I refuse a Miss Marple lookalike? At the end of the evening, I am not sure how, but she had uncovered the whole sorry tale of the events of the past six months by making observations and not exactly asking questions. She didn't issue platitudes or the usual comments about time healing. I felt comforted if that is the correct word. I, such a private person have never revealed so much of myself to someone I didn't know. I think she should have been recruited by MI6 as an interrogator, certainly could have given George Smiley a run for his money. I slept through the night for the first time in six months.

I have established a pattern for my days. An early morning walk down the hillside to swim in the turquoise sea. After breakfast a walk and some exploring, perhaps some reading or writing in the afternoon then join our hosts and other guests for dinner if I feel strong enough.

At dawn on the first morning after my arrival, I found myself swimming out towards the horizon; it seemed an easy escape, a way to drift into oblivion. Then I looked back over my shoulder towards the shore. The sun was just painting the beach and edge of the water rosy pink and water kicked up by my feet sparkled like precious jewels in the crisp morning air. I found that I wasn't yet ready to leave this, unexpectedly at times, beautiful world.

Lavinia, my dear sister, I thank you as always for your support over the years particularly over this bleak time in my life. I am slowly recovering and you have strengthened me.

Last evening while flicking through old Visitors Books, I saw an entry by a Lavinia Buchanan and a George Harrison. That wasn't you by any chance the summer you went missing?

Blessings,

Charles.

30 September 1975

Dear Charles

How good to hear from you and that you are gradually finding some peace in the secluded retreat that is Paros.

How observant you are! Yes that was my signature – it was a magical summer for me when I 'dropped out of life' for a few months. George and I laughed and lived each day without thought of the future and what lay ahead. Both of us needed time out from pressures of people and life and it set us strongly on the successful path of our own chosen professions. Not together, but we were there for each other in the right place at the right time.

Now tell me Charles, have you been writing? If you can without putting pressure on yourself I feel it will help.

Give my very kind regards to Stefan and Ana. They helped me restore my faith in human kind and I hope they have done the same for you.

Let me know when you are ready to come back and I will arrange with Mrs. Banks to get things ready for you.

Take care, I think of you often,
With love,
Lavinia

10th October, 1975
Dear Lavinia

I feel I am ready to face the world again. I have booked my ticket to arrive at Heathrow Monday week at 12noon.

I would like to take advantage of your penchant for organizing things and ask you to arrange with the Funeral Director to collect the bodies of Susanna, Phillip and Adriana from the

Mortuary; and fix a time for a funeral service at St Cuthbert's in Carter Road for the following Friday.

I know that people found it strange I didn't have the funeral after the accident but I couldn't face it. I thought I would lose my mind. Now I feel strong enough to give them the funeral they deserve and decide what I want to do with the rest of my life without them. They will always be with me, birthdays, anniversaries, Christmas. They made their individual mark on the world in their own way, and I will carry them in my heart all of my life.

Again Lavinia I must thank you for being so strong and helping me during this survival part of my journey, and to finally face what happened and honour their memory by continuing to live.

With love
Charles.

THE END

THE WELL TRAVELLED
SUITCASE

'So this is where I end my long life, waiting for a truck to take me to the dump.' The elderly suitcase sighed. As the morning sun rose over the hills surrounding the quiet suburban village, the suitcase settled more comfortably against the tree where she had been dumped along with the rest of unwanted rubbish.

She dreamed of how her life began in Paris in a fashionable shop on the Champs Élysées as the latest design of the Louis Vuitton Brand. Placed in the centre of a beautiful window display, she waited for someone to come along and buy her and so begin a fabulous life of travel.

Forty minutes after she was placed in the window, a long car drew up outside the beautiful shop and out stepped the glamorous Princess Marie Chantal Louise and her Godmother the

Grand Duchess from a small but very wealthy Principality. They were staying in Paris preparing for an eagerly awaited trip to New York.

An hour later after drinking a glass of champagne and choosing the latest trunks and suitcases, including the little case in the window, the ladies swept out to go back to their hotel and oversee their maids pack for them.

From that day on the beautiful hand crafted small case travelled to many different destinations; never far from her owner's possession. She was either being packed or unpacked by the Princess's personal maid, Josie. When not in use the case was covered by a soft cloth and stored carefully to protect her beautiful cover.

After years of care and attention, travelling, and being admired, suddenly it all came to an end. Princess Marie Chantal eloped with her mother's butler and the little case was left behind. Josie, her personal maid, who had always loved the case, received it as a going away present when she left the household to take up a position as a junior typist with a major newspaper in London. She had been given a reference and introduction to the editor by the Grand Duchess's brother who owned part of the newspaper.

In the evenings, Josie began to write her account of life as a Ladies Maid with aristocratic families. Then she stored her writing in the beautiful little Louis Vuitton case.

Several years later Josie fell madly in love with one of the sub-editors at the paper. He proposed and her writing was put to one side if not forgotten. She and Stuart were busy planning a low-key wedding and packing as they were emigrating to Melbourne in Australia, leaving behind the turmoil that was Europe to begin a new life, sailing shortly after their marriage.

The Louis Vuitton case was hastily wrapped and packed in a tea-chest with other larger items and just before embarkation sent to the ship to be stored in the hold until they arrived in Melbourne.

So began a very different life in Australia, building a life with Stuart and her growing family. From time to time over the years, Josie took out the little case, gazed at the contents, added some more notes, and sighed over memories of her time spent as a young personal maid to the Princess, witnessing the intrigues, glamorous parties, affairs. She found it difficult to believe that was part of her world when she was much younger.

Josie thought about writing that novel she had planned before she met Stuart, but then life and her family took priority and the idea was shelved once again. Eventually the case was relegated to the loft and forgotten.

Decades later, after Josie's funeral, the family returned home to find the house had been ransacked and whoever had broken in had even gone into the loft and cleared all that might be worth anything. The police said that a well-organized gang had been operating throughout the State and were thought to be from New Zealand.

A few weeks later, in a quiet suburb on the outskirts of the city of Auckland, a large shipping container was unpacked with the proceeds of countless burglaries carried out in Victoria, Australia. Coming across the old rather dusty case the gang leader gave a cursory glance inside and tossed it aside to be thrown out for the rubbish collection next day.

Early next morning, Jim, who raised funds for a local charity, was driving down the streets where the unwanted items were put out for the annual inorganic collection. He sometimes picked up things which could bring in a few dollars and the money was put to good use. Jim saw the little case almost buried under other rubbish and leaves from the tree above. He drew in his breath. It looked a bit like the photograph of an early Louis Vuitton case that he and his girlfriend Marie had been looking at in an old 1930's magazine at the weekend.

Could it possibly be Louis Vuitton? Jim stopped, picked up the little case, dusted off the rubbish and placed it carefully in the back of his van.

Marie loved vintage items and collected whatever she could find at weekend markets when she could. She worked in the local library, belonged to a writer's group and her stories reflected the era that fascinated her. The 1920's and '30's.

After dinner that night, Jim said, "I think I have a surprise for you." He cleared the table and placed the little case on a piece of newspaper. "I thought I recognized this when I was doing my rounds this morning, thrown out for rubbish collection. What do you think? Is it like the photos in the magazine we were looking at over the weekend?"

A gasp of delight from Marie confirmed his guess was right.

"I don't believe it, early Louis Vuitton, it's beautiful - Jim you are a genius!" she flung her arms round his neck and kissed him. "I wonder where it came from."

Opening the case Marie stroked the beautiful lining, a little the worse for wear having been somewhere damp. She felt something behind the silk, and carefully feeling for an opening, drew out an envelope and then three more. Jim and Marie sat for a moment gazing at the four bulky envelopes, packed with sheets of lined paper filled with writing in ink that was fading. "This looks like a long evening ahead of reading, I'll make a pot of tea," said Jim.

Marie was already looking at dates to see where to begin. It was early morning before Jim and Marie finished reading the incredible stories written almost a century ago.

A year later Marie's best-seller "The Well Travelled Suitcase" was launched. Josie's well-documented insight into life with the Princess and the people she surrounded herself with was perfect material for the novel she had always dreamed of writing.

Marie and Jim had talked with legal publishing experts to ensure that there would not be any problem with plagiarism but it was accepted the notes were written over 70 years earlier so all was well and safe for Marie to adapt the stories for her novel.

In the front of the book Marie acknowledged Josie and hoped she would have been happy that the notes she made of her life and experiences were being avidly read and enjoyed. The public's timeless interest in programmes like Upstairs Downstairs and Downton Abbey meant the book was already into a third printing and there was talk of a television series.

When Marie was on a world tour promoting her book she was invited to Louis Vuitton Head Office in Paris where they restored the little case to its former glory. They wanted to buy the case back but Marie refused. The case meant so much to her and it was somehow a connection to Josie. The beautiful boutique made do with a photograph of Marie with the case and a copy of her book.

In the lovely home, bought with the proceeds of sales from "The Well Travelled Suitcase", where Jim and Marie now lived; the little suitcase which had been picked up amongst rubbish in a leafy suburban street was in pride of place in the study placed on a small 1930's table. Marie was currently working on a sequel and her agent was having discussions with Hollywood about the possibility of a movie. It looked like there was some more travelling ahead for the suitcase.

THE END

MORNING ROUNDS – MRS JONES

The doors to Ward 7 trauma ward opened and in bustled doctors, students and attendant medical staff to carry out morning rounds. Another busy night in the large city hospital and as well as A & E coping with the usual round of stupid accidents, there had been a multiple motorway crash and a major fire in a nearby apartment block. As more and more patients arrived, trolleys were being used for new patients as they came in and lined up in hallways. All the hospitals in the city were overcrowded with the emergency.

Ward 7 post-operative ward was full to overflowing; the Junior Registrars, doctors and nurses had been on 15 hour shifts, running on adrenaline; unsure when they would be relieved and trying very hard to keep alert.

Halfway down the ward the medical staff came to a bed where a woman lay with a drip in one hand, the other hand restlessly plucking at the sheet.

Picking up the chart clipped at the end of the bed, Doctor Maxwell said, "Good Morning, Mrs. Jones."

"Morning," came the reply in a shaky voice.

"About time you lot came to check on us," said a voice from the next bed.

"We'll be with you in a moment, we are just seeing Mrs. Jones," said the Staff Nurse.

"I'm Mrs. Jones," both women said in unison.

Swiftly one of the medical staff picked up the chart from the next bed. "Are you Mrs. Tessa Jones?"

"Yep, that's me," came the answer from the first bed.

"No that's my name," came a reply from the next bed.

Silence hung over the group, then they went into a huddle and scrutinized both charts. What were the chances of there being two Mrs. Tessa Jones, both 48, both admitted after the motorway crash? Both heads were bandaged, both had arms in slings.

Screens were quickly drawn round the beds and a nurse dispatched to find the Administrator and Manager of the hospital.

Trying not to alarm both women their details were gone over again and double checked. One had been in a car that had been tailgated by a bus; the other had been a passenger on the bus.

One had multiple fractures and the other a ruptured spleen, injuries to her head and a broken arm. Both had been unconscious and covered in blood. Details of both women had been taken from their handbags which had been placed in the ambulance taking them to hospital after they had been pulled from the wreckage around them. Staff had tried to contact their next of kin but as yet no one had come forward. The handbags must have been mixed up.

While a student nurse stayed with each woman, reassuring them, asking for more details and taking vital signs, senior consultants and administrative staff were trying to sort out what happened amongst the chaos in A & E last night. It looked like the wrong Mrs. Jones had her spleen removed.

Both women were taken into private rooms and rechecked from top to toe. Never had a more thorough medical check been carried out. Mrs.

Tessa Jones number one, (she was two months older) turned out to have a heart murmur. Mrs. Tessa Jones number two, had a raging chest infection.

The medical misadventure was hastily corrected; the correct spleen removed exhausted staff admonished for the mistakes.

The two Mrs. Jones's ended up in a small ward together, recovering and enjoying the unexpected extra attention. Lying back and replying weakly to enquiries about how they were feeling. "I'm a little better thank you, but could just manage another cup of tea and a piece of cake."

On their own the two Mrs. Tessa Jones' formed a firm friendship, the older Mrs. Jones saying, "They have stuffed up somewhere along the way and are trying to cover up, but I reckon we'll take everything that is due to us. We deserve it."

"I suspect you're right Tess old girl, make them sweat a bit, still at least they didn't take the wrong leg off." And the two new friends went into hoots of laughter and dunked another biscuit into their satisfyingly strong cups of tea.

THE END

BANANA SPLIT

They sat in anxious silence watching carefully every move that Mr. Johnston made. The four children had been working hard all morning, now was the moment they had all been waiting for.

During the summer holidays they had rattled around the town, gone out to Judy's Uncle's farm, played ball, waded in the river and generally had the time of their 10 year old lives. Now they needed some money. ET was showing at the local picture house and they desperately wanted to see the movie. No one had any money and pocket money wasn't part of their young lives.

Bill, the ideas man of the gang, suggested they smarten themselves up and go to see the owner of the local Milk Bar Mr. Johnston, to see if he had any jobs that needed doing. Bill went in first as he had the confidence to talk with grown-ups.

"Morning, Mr. Johnston," the bright faced young Bill said.

"Good morning to you too son," smiled Mr. Johnston, "What can I do for you?"

"Well sir, it is really more what I can do for you," answered Bill earnestly. "You see me and my friends want to earn some money for a special project, we work hard and don't charge much." He screwed his face up anxiously waiting for Mr. Johnston's answer.

Mr. Johnston hid a smile. "Well as it happens my assistant can't come in today and I do need the store room cleared out and tidied. Are you sure you and your young friends are strong enough to work hard for the four hours I need without stopping?"

"Oh yes Sir," beamed Bill. "We are reliable, hard workers and I am sure you will be satisfied with the job we do." He had his fingers crossed behind his back, but he already could see them all sitting in a row in the picture house watching ET.

"Bring your colleagues in and we will discuss terms," said Mr. Johnson.

Bill swaggered a little as he went outside. "We got the job," he said proudly, "now we have to go in and discuss terms." Three collective jaws dropped at the words 'discuss terms' but their backs straightened a little.

Mr. Johnston eyed the four anxious little faces in front of him. "Mmm, do you think you are reliable and strong enough to work steadily for four hours and do a good job?"

"Oh yes Sir," chorused the four skinny little figures in front of him.

"If you do a good job and carry out all the tasks on my list, then you will get four dollars each. That is one dollar per hour, how does that sound?"

Three young mouths opened to say, "yes, that's great."

But Bill stepped in and said firmly, "Aw! Mr. Johnston, it's hard work in the heat so we would need a drink. Could you add a soda to our pay?" Bill screwed his face up, twisted his hands behind his back wondering if he had gone too far.

But Mr. Johnston smiled. "Well I will come in after two hours and if you are doing a good job, you can have 10 minutes break and a soda each."

Four delighted faces beamed up at him. They quickly followed Mr. Johnston into the store room behind the Soda Parlour and he showed them where the boxes needed to be stacked for taking away, where the big brooms were for sweeping up the sidewalk, shelves to be restocked, and other boxes unpacked.

He went back into the store as the bell rang to let him know another customer wanted attention. Quietly keeping an eye on the children over the morning he was impressed with Bill's skills for organizing the others. Two hours passed and the store room was beginning to resemble the neat place he liked it to be. He came in with a tray holding four larges glasses of creaming soda with a scoop of ice cream, long straws and spoons sticking out.

Four dirty faces looked up at him gratefully. Silence reigned as the sodas were devoured.

"You're all doing a good job, I am very pleased so far, carry on and in two hours I will see you with your pay." Mr. Johnston took the glasses and spoons back, licked almost clean.

"Oh!" sighed Judy, "that was the best thing I've ever tasted."

"Come on, let's finish the job, and when we collect our pay let me talk, I have an idea," said Bill firmly.

By the time midday arrived Mr. Johnston stood with his hands on his hips and surveyed the store room, shelves stacked, everything neat tidy and swept clean. "Well I have to admit I didn't think you kids would do such a bang up job. Let's go to the store and I'll get your pay."

"Thank you Mr. Johnston," said Bill, "can I ask you something?"

"Sure Bill," answered Mr. Johnston, wondering what this smart youngster was going to come out with.

"Well as we do a good job I was thinking we might ask around for other jobs," Bill stuttered a little, "I was wondering if you would recommend us?"

"Well sure I will. I am very pleased with what you have done and if I ever need some help again I will be glad to ask you and your team." Mr. Johnston smiled at the four tired, dirty young people.

"One more thing, Mr. Johnston," asked Bill pointing to a picture over the counter. "How much does that cost?"

"Why, that's a Super Dooper Dish Bill, it costs four dollars."

Bill went into a huddle with his friends then faced Mr. Johnston again. "Could we please have one dish and four spoons, and then you pay us three dollars each?"

They sat anxiously on stools carefully watching every move the store keeper made. They saw the most enormous Banana Split grow in front of them, with chocolate sauce, whipped cream, ice cream and four cherries on top.

Sitting at a table with a long spoon each of them took a turn to have a spoonful and enjoy the most delicious Banana Split they had ever tasted. Slowly the confection disappeared, every mouthful savoured until the plate was clean and shiny. Wow! What a day! A job done well, pay and two delicious treats; then tomorrow the picture house and ET. What a wonderful end to the summer holidays.

Twenty years later Bill and his friends who had gone their separate ways after school but still kept in touch, met at the funeral of Mr. Johnston. They remembered the day they had earned their first pay, learned some good lessons and how nothing had ever compared to the taste of that Banana Split.

THE TWIG

"Is it a big tree Nan?" Mickey was looking at his grandmother in a puzzled fashion.

Kathleen was looking after her grandson while her son Joe and daughter-in-law were at Starship Hospital with their little daughter Bridie. The doctor who had suspected meningitis sent them off early that morning. To distract Mickey and herself she had suggested they go up to the attic and look at the Family Tree. It was in a big sea chest that had belonged to her sea captain grandfather and had amused herself, brothers and sisters and her children over the years. It was full of maps, family photographs, treasures belonging to past generations and the wonderful huge chart of the family tree.

"No Mickey, it isn't a tree that grows in the garden but a family tree which shows all the family down the years. Grandpas, Grandmas, uncles, aunts, cousins, your Mam and Dad, it grows every time another member of the family is born."

They climbed the stairs to the packed room with a lifetime of memories and at the back was the big wooden chest. Kathleen lifted the lid and carefully took a box out of the chest. "Maybe it will stop me worrying about the baby," she said to herself.

Five minutes later they were seated at the big dining room table and Kathleen gently took out the thick sheets of paper carefully begun by Great Uncle Paddy all those many years ago. Every generation there was always one family member who took on the job of adding the marriages, deaths and recording the births of the growing family on the chart.

Mickey had good concentration for a seven-year-old and waited patiently for his Nana to tell him about the Family Tree. He was secretly pleased it wasn't a real tree; it might have broken the roof if it had grown too big. He had a vivid imagination.

Kathleen carefully unfolded the papers, putting them in the correct order. "Look Mickey, right at the top is your Great, Great, Great

Grandpa James and Grandma Margaret Dinsmore who were born in Ireland but came out to New Zealand 150 years ago."

They looked at each branch, then Kathleen said, "Now then, see that new branch Mickey? There is your Mam and your Daddy, underneath is your name Michel Joseph Dinsmore and the date you were born, beside you is little Bridget Mary Dinsmore and her date of birth.

"All those branches, Nana," said Mickey, "does that make me a twig, and Bridie will be a twiglet." He whooped with seven-year-old boy's humour. Kathleen swooped him up in her arms. "Ah Michael Og, you're a delight." Her heart lifted with love for her grandson.

"What's an Og, Nana?" he asked, attention fastening on an unfamiliar word.

"It's an Irish word meaning little, perhaps a Daddy would be called Michael and his son Michael Og, so people would know who they were talking about, but mostly it is a term of affection, my Mickey Og."

Mickey was looking back at the chart and suddenly asked, "Why are we at the top of the tree again Nana?"

"You can't be," said Kathleen, "it must be a mistake." Putting on her glasses she saw very faintly a tiny branch with small script. Her heart gave a lurch. Why had she never see it before when she looked at it with first her grandmother, parents and then her children?

Michael Joseph Dinsmore aged seven, died as a result of a tragic accident, and Bridget Mary Dinsmore died of a diphtheria epidemic 18 months old and dated today's date but 80 years earlier. The ghosts of dozens of Irish ancestors walked over her grave. She shivered and folded up the papers carefully.

"Let's have a cup of tea and go for a walk in Cornwall Park Mickey, now the rain has stopped," said Kathleen, trying to distract Mickey and herself from the coincidence of reading the dates of the deaths of two children with the same names of her beloved grandchildren, 80 years earlier.

"Yeah! Let's go," said Mickey. "We can have a swing, collect cones and see the sheep." He was always a busy boy.

They wrapped up warmly, for although it was now sunny, there was a cold wind. Cornwall Park was always a delight no matter what the weather. They walked through the trees, patting dogs, marveling at the trees with autumn leaves on one side and the other with burgeoning pink blossoms after a few days of sunny weather.

Running after Mickey Kathleen began to feel better, and out in the crisp fresh air she began to put out of her mind that two small children with the same names as her grandchildren had died on today's date 80 years ago. Ignoring the chill on her neck she pointed out a playful dog to her grandson.

They had come out of the trees and were heading up the road to the old house and the kiosk to buy an ice cream. No matter what the weather, Mickey always loved ice cream. He was dancing ahead, waving a stick like a sword at an imaginary lion. He shouted that it was going to eat her. Suddenly he saw a small dog sitting on the other side of the road and turned to run towards it.

Kathleen felt a roaring in her head, as suddenly the background changed, the trees were younger, smaller, the road was rocky and unpaved, and a car which was bearing down on them was a vintage model. She tried to run but was hampered, no longer wearing jeans, instead her legs were encased in a long tweed skirt. She had on a restricting long coat and hat pulled down over her face. What was happening?

Everything was in slow motion and seemed a long way away. All at once she felt herself yell "NO, NO, not again!" She threw herself forward, once more her legs encased in jeans, scooped Michael up in her arms and fell in the gutter on the other side of the road, dazed and holding tight to her grandson.

"Oh! Sorry! Sorry," gasped a young girl dressed in 20's style clothes driving her vintage car to a rally. She jumped down from the high front seat, her passengers white-faced in the backt.

"Yes, yes, we're fine, just a bit shaken, nothing an ice cream won't fix," said Kathleen reassuringly. She wanted them gone, to think over what had happened and calm her thudding heart.

"Please Nana, you're squeezing me," said Mickey in a subdued voice.

"Oh! Sorry my pet, I got such a fright, are you ok?" she said anxiously, looking into her darling grandson's face.

"Yes I'm alright. Sorry Nan, I shouldn't have run on the road."

"No, Michael Dinsmore, that is not what you do, you've taken years off my life. What would I have told your poor Mam and Dad?

Promise me you will always look before crossing a road and only go when it is safe." Kathleen gave him another hug.

"I will, Nana, I'm sorry."

"Well then, I think we can treat ourselves to a Rush Munro ice cream, don't you think?"

"Yes please Nana Og," grinned Mickey. "Og is a word of affection Nan." He hurried up to check out the flavours of the ice cream.

Seated on the warm stone steps across from the restaurant and old house, Kathleen with her Lemon and Gin ice cream and Mickey with double chocolate, they looked down at the trees and people walking and the beautiful park and each went over their own thoughts.

Was that how young Michael from 80 years ago had died? Was he run over by a car, his grandmother with her long heavy clothes unable to reach and save him in time? She wondered who would believe her if she tried to tell them. Was it a coincidence, or was young Mickey being saved by his Great-Great Grandmother who had been unable to save her young Michael? Whatever happened, thank God for coincidence, psychic insight, family trees and jeans! But what about Bridie?

A familiar roaring filled her ears, and this time she was looking down on a little iron cot. Two weeping young people and a doctor in old fashioned clothes, looking down on the dead baby. Again Kathleen found her voice and shouted "No!! No!"

The picture changed and the ward where little Bridie had been admitted came into focus. Anya and Joe were smiling and looking at the doctor who was holding a wide awake and solemn-faced Bridie. Everything was alright. Thank God!

"You're squeezing me again Nana, what's wrong?" asked an anxious Mickey.

"Not a thing my pet, everything is wonderful. Why don't we go up and see Bridie in hospital, I am sure she is better and I have a feeling everything is going to be grand."

As Kathleen fastened Mickey into his car seat, he showed her a little twig with leaves from the past season on one side and a few pink blossoms for the new season on the other. "A present for the little twiglet," he smiled.

"Good boy, what a lovely idea." Smiling, she shut the door and they drove to the hospital. She thought she had better write an account of this day and put it with the Family Tree papers

71

and maybe when Mickey was grown and had a family of his own he would remember.

Twenty five years later and two weeks after Kathleen's funeral, and one week after his baby daughter was born, Michael opened an envelope that his beloved Nana had left for him.

Inside was a dried little twig wrapped in acid free tissue paper, the twig he had brought for his little sister when she was in Starship Hospital, and inside a letter that Kathleen had written 25 years ago after the family had brought his sister Bridie home.

He read the letter twice and checked the date, before dropping the letter with his grandmother's familiar hand writing on the table and thinking of that day in the park all those years ago. He remembered in sharp detail the events of the day, finding the faint record of two children with the same names as his sister and himself, the dates. The family tree, different types of trees in the park with leaves from the past season and new blossom for the future. Sitting in the gutter with Nana holding him tightly, the taste of chocolate ice cream. "I don't believe it," he muttered.

"Believe it," Kathleen's voice sounded in his head. "You and Bridie are still here with your own families now."

Another little Kathleen Ann Dinsmore. He smiled at a photograph of his Nana holding his hand. They were smiling at each other at some long-forgotten joke.

"Watch over your namesake Nana Og, and thank you for giving me my life and allowing me to add my children's names to the Family Tree."

THE END

THE UNFINISHED DANCE

Poppy was about to shut up the Vintage Shop she was managing for her cousin Clare when a truck with a builder's logo on the side, drew up with a screech of brakes. The driver a tall, tanned, fair haired young man jumped out, easily picked up an old trunk on the back of the truck, shouldered the door open, and came into the shop.

"I'm not too late, am I?" he grinned. He put the trunk on the ground and explained. "I'm renovating an old house on the outskirts of town, found this in the attic and thought of your shop. The new owners told me to burn any rubbish, but I remembered my sister had got a great dress here for a party and I thought you might like the clothes. I think they are from the 1920's."

"Fabulous," said Poppy, smiling back at him as his grin was infectious. "That's very kind; can I pay you something for them?"

He laughed. "No thanks, I feel they are too interesting to be burned and deserve another party or two. I think there is some history there."

He rushed out of the shop, jumped in his truck and roared off with a wave.

Poppy locked up, pulled down the blinds and spent the next few hours entranced at the contents of the trunk. They had been beautifully wrapped and somehow survived all the years of being locked away without fading or disintegrating. She came across some clothes which appeared to have watermarks on them. Suddenly Poppy felt the clothes had been packed away by someone who was crying. She sat back on her heels and wondered why the clothes had been put away and forgotten, as most of them looked fairly unworn.

At the very bottom of the trunk lay an old fashioned gramophone complete with horn; separately packed and wrapped in beautiful, bright, fine, silk scarves was a pile of old records. Poppy unpacked them carefully, wound up the gramophone, put on a record and the shop was filled with the joyous sound of the Charleston. It was infectious music and she couldn't help swaying in time as she went into the tiny kitchen at the back to put the kettle on and make some tea.

She smiled as she thought of the beautiful flapper dresses, long strings of beads, head bands, feathers and tiny bags on chains. Men's evening suits with tails, wonderful shirts some slightly yellowing with age. Bow ties and shoes, fantastic shoes with straps and heels to dance the night away.

The music was winding down and Poppy became aware of laughter and voices from the shop! She went through and saw some of the clothes from the hangers had gone and two ethereal young people were jitterbugging in time to the music.

"Oh! Wind it up again darling, we haven't finished dancing, and we can't hold the handle! "A young blonde girl waved her ghostly hand at Poppy to show her she could see through it.

"Who... who are you?" she stuttered, wondering how on earth anyone could have got through the double locked door of the shop. Somehow she wasn't afraid of these young people but began to realize they must be ghosts as she could clearly see the shop walls behind them.

"This is Jack and I'm Primrose, thank you for unpacking our clothes. We have been earth bound for nearly 90 years. Jack asked me to marry him at the last of the summer season balls and we were planning to tell our families and friends when we had finished dancing the night away."

Jack continued. "Sadly Monty waved his arms too energetically and knocked the candelabra over, the curtains caught fire, and as we were all a bit squiffy with champagne everyone was burnt to a crisp."

Poppy gasped at the description of the fabulous night ending so tragically. Jack and Primrose looked sad and Primrose said, "My brother and our pals died that night too, and we never got to see our families and tell them our marvelous news or say goodbye."

"Monty didn't mean it darling," Jack comforted. "We now have the opportunity to finish our dance and then get on with our eternal rest." He stared hard at Poppy. "What is your name? You do look familiar."

"I was thinking the same," laughed Poppy. "It was like looking in a mirror when I saw

Primrose only she has that lovely bob haircut and mine is long. Maybe we are long lost cousins!"

Primrose hooted with giggles. "What a lark if we are connected. Please Poppy wind the gramophone up again, we have a lot of dancing to catch up with."

Soon the little shop was ringing with the sound of Jitterbug, Jazz, Bebop and Charleston. Jack and Primrose showed her the steps and soon she was dancing as if she spent all her spare Saturday nights at the local hop. Laughter rang out; Poppy hadn't had so much fun for ages.

When they had gone through the complete repertoire of music Jack began to look through some of the dance cards and invitations. "Primrose look," he said, "your Mama must have packed up all last season's invitations, wasn't that sweet? Our families were devastated Poppy, we felt awful watching them grieve and not being able to comfort them and tell them our news or say goodbye."

Primrose suddenly shivered. "What if those ghastly people who bought the old home had burnt all our things? We would never have finished our dance and moved on."

"It's almost time to go Poppy, thanks so much for being such a pal helping us finish our final dance and taking good care of our things, it has all been such fun," Primrose pealed with laughter. "Come on Jack, the dance is over; we have just one more mystery to solve before we catch up with Monty and the others."

She paused. "I say Poppy, invite that young man who found our trunk over for tea, see if he can dance. I think he may be able to fulfill our dream and yours. And he looks a lot like my Jack!" She blew Poppy a kiss, Jack sketched a half salute and the figures gradually disappeared leaving their clothes on the floor and a faint smell of violets in the air.

Poppy felt like pinching herself. Did this evening really happen? Was she dreaming about the last few hours learning to dance as they did in the early '20's? Seeing ghosts or at least spirits which couldn't rest until they had completed what they started before dying so suddenly and tragically? She was suddenly filled with unexpected delight and happiness – wondering if she had really helped these young people move on after almost 90 years. But what did Poppy mean about another mystery to solve?

Putting dust covers carefully over all the beautiful clothes, she locked up, and as usual shook the door to make sure it was shut tight.

Then she went home to the little flat she had moved into so happily two years ago with James. James – she realized that she hadn't thought of him all day, now that was progress.

Next morning when Poppy opened up the shop she found a card in the door.

Jason Frobisher, Builder, Renovations and Repairs.

Scribbled underneath was a note. *I'd like to hear what was in the Trunk. Can we meet for coffee? Call me. Jason.*

Poppy heard the echo of a familiar giggle and a smell of violets drifted round the tiny shop.

"Good morning Primrose," said Poppy, "I know you are there." She smiled in the general direction of the ceiling.

She wound up the gramophone, put on the now familiar tunes. "I wonder if Jason can dance?" she mused. Picking up the phone she dialed the number on the card. She was just about to hang up when the phone was answered. "Hi Jason, it's Poppy from the Vintage Shop, is this a good time to talk?"

"No it isn't," came a gruff reply and he disconnected the call.

Poppy felt her heart sink, embarrassed, then angry at the response. He had seemed so nice and friendly. He had asked her to contact him. How could she have got it so wrong?

She automatically went through the process of opening the shop feeling as if she had been doused in cold water. Since her relationship with James had finished a year or so ago, Poppy had not been out with anyone else. The emotional damage of catering to a selfish demanding man had stopped her from being open to accepting invitations to dinner or the movies. Her friends had tried to introduce her to 'suitable prospects' but she wasn't interested.

James had humiliated her. After three years together, going on holiday, finally moving in together sharing the tiny flat she had found and made into a home for them, one Friday night he had come home from work and told her he was moving out. They really weren't suited - she must have known that. He had found a girl he was really in love with and they were moving to London.

Poppy had been absolutely gobsmacked. She had broken into sobs as the door slammed behind James and he left with his backpack, suitcases, the CD's (most of which she had bought) and the beautiful throw she had bought when they were holidaying in Spain. Maybe they had got into a bit of a routine, but they still had fun. What had she done wrong? It must have been her fault.

Then she remembered the long passionate love they had made a few nights earlier. They had lingered over a beautiful dinner Poppy had prepared for their anniversary, with several bottles of his favourite wine. Afterwards they had fallen asleep in each other's arms. How could he be in love with someone else and make love to her?

It had taken ages for Poppy to begin to pick up the pieces of her life again. Her cousin Clare who owned the Vintage Shop had helped enormously. She included her in outings, taking her places and out of her routine with James. Then Clare asked her to look after the shop when she went on holiday with her husband and one-year-old daughter and Poppy had jumped at the chance. Something completely different; taking unpaid leave from her administrative job in the library, she threw herself into a completely different working environment. She was dealing with happy people who were looking for something exceptional to wear for a special party.

Instead of working out statistics and updating catalogues, she enjoyed arranging racks of lovely old clothes, making sure they were clean and pressed, finding just the right outfit for the right person. Life was looking up and she felt finally she was over James. He was just another selfish male sod.

Meeting Jason briefly, a man she had thought was different, kind and thoughtful, who had gone to the trouble of saving the box of beautiful clothes instead of burning them, had raised a flicker of interest. It appeared she was wrong. Good thing she hadn't gone out with him and perhaps grown to more than like him.

Poppy filled a bucket of soapy water, pulled on rubber gloves and began spring cleaning areas of the shop which hadn't been touched for a while. Like many other women Poppy found it a good way to get rid of frustration and being made to feel inadequate – scrub everything in sight.

Several hours later when the tiny shop was polished and cleaned to her satisfaction, she sat down with a feeling of a job well done. With a cup of coffee and a lemon and poppy seed muffin to tuck into, she took a well-deserved break. Just as she had taken a most unladylike large bite, the phone rang. Emptying her mouthful into her napkin, "Mmm! 'allo, yes," she mumbled.

"Now Poppy, that's not a very professional way to answer the phone of our select establishment." Clare's laughing voice came down the phone.

"Oh! Clare, thank goodness it's you, I'd just taken a huge bite of a muffin and my mouth was full! And I did think it was someone else!"

"Sounds interesting, now this someone else wouldn't be of the male persuasion would they? Tell me more," said Clare teasingly.

"I'll regale you with the story when you come home. Now tell me are you, Mike and little Sally having fun?" Poppy changed the subject.

"It is so wonderful," sighed Clare. "Mike and I are very grateful that you stepped into the breach, this break is just what we need after the past few years, you are a treasure Poppy. We feel renewed and re-energized. Bless you darling, take care and see you in a couple of weeks." The phone spluttered and Clare rang off.

Poppy felt a bit tearful when she put the phone down. She was very happy for Clare and Mike but it emphasized how alone she felt. It would be so good to have someone to talk with, put their arm around her and have a cuddle when life got a bit stressful. For a moment she even missed James. In the beginning he had been kind, thoughtful and appreciated her. On reflection it didn't last long, they always did what he wanted to do, what movies to see, where they went out and with his friends not hers. In fact she had been a doormat. She gave herself a little shake and reminded herself that having the wrong person in her life was not better than having no one at all.

After lunch the shop was quite busy, as it was party season and vintage clothes were all the rage. Poppy enjoyed matching up the right outfit to the person who was looking for that 'something special.'

One young woman asked, "Are you a professional stylist? My sister hired a professional who charged the earth for something gorgeous to wear to her firm's annual dinner, I think you do a much better job." Another delighted customer left the shop.

"Yes, you are doing an amazing job." An amused voice came from behind one of the clothes racks. A tall dark haired man approached the counter holding up one of the outfits from Primrose and Jack's trunk.

"Where did you get these clothes? These are the genuine article all right," he said.

Poppy opened her mouth to give him an abridged version of how the clothes came to the shop. But something stopped her; the smell of violets was in the air and she felt protective of the young people she had danced with so energetically a few nights ago; or at least their spirits.

She laughed and said, "Oh! We never reveal our sources!" making a joke out of the reply.

The dark eyes went cold for a moment, and then he smiled again. "Well if you do remember or find out, I'll pay for them all. I'm a collector and items like these are getting harder to find." He held out a simple embossed card with just the name Clifford Anstace and a phone number. "Anyway I'll buy this one now, how much?" he said reaching for his wallet.

Poppy began to say what she had priced it at and suddenly felt a pinch. She jumped. It was the suit Jack had worn.

"I'm sorry, it isn't for sale, someone asked me to hold it for them and I haven't got round to taking it off the rack," Poppy said firmly. Somehow she didn't want to sell Jack's suit to this man, she had taken an instant dislike to him. She wondered if it had been Primrose who had pinched her.

He looked searchingly at her and Poppy knew he didn't believe her. He opened his mouth to speak but Poppy hurriedly said, "I certainly will call you if I find out from the owner where the clothes came from. Now if you don't mind I am closing for an hour as I have some things to sort out and I am on my own." She realized she was gabbling as she steered the man towards the door, closed it firmly and dropped the lock.

Poppy found she was shaking and couldn't understand why this man had disturbed her so much. She went to the rack where she had hung the clothes from the trunk then remembered she had put them in the back room to press them. She must have forgotten Jack's suit.

Checking round the shop before closing she wondered why the man wanted that particular suit as there were at least two others of similar design, although not of the same beautiful material and style.

Suddenly she stopped what she was doing, collected all of Primrose and Jack's clothes, wrapped the gramophone up in some old clothes which wouldn't have sold, and put them in the boot of her car.

She locked up then drove home wondering what on earth had made her do what she did. Maybe she had inherited her Irish Grandmother's intuition. After unpacking the car and carefully storing the beautiful clothes and gramophone in her bedroom, Poppy poured a glass of Pinot Noir, popped one of the frozen dinners Clare had thoughtfully provided into the oven and checked her answer machine. There was only one message. Nothing was said, just silence for a few moments then the sound of a phone clicking off. Slightly unnerved she took another sip of wine, then dismissed it. The oven timer pinged dinner was ready.

Next morning Poppy was singing along with the radio as she turned into the street where The Vintage Shop stood, arriving early to look over some more clothes she had recently sourced. She went into shock as she saw the front door smashed and swinging open. A young constable was standing outside talking into his radio link to the station. Poppy rushed over. "What's happened?" she gasped in a frightened voice. "I'm running the shop for the owners."

"We had a call from one of the neighbours in the new flats across the road," the young constable said. "He noticed a car cruising up and down after you had shut the shop last evening, and this morning early he heard the sound of breaking glass, saw what was happening and called us. He is recovering from an accident and has appointed himself 'neighbour watch'. Good job too, just as we turned into the street we saw a car speeding off, we have a call out with the description. We haven't gone in yet as we're trying to track down the owners, so perhaps you can come in if you are up to it and we can check if anything has been stolen." He pushed the door for Poppy and followed her into the shop.

She explained the owners were away and she was looking after the business for them and that they were family. She would take responsibility for enquiries as she didn't want to upset their holiday.

"It looks like opportunists or vandals," said the constable. "Let us have a report if anything is missing and I would get someone in to fix the door and lock as soon as possible." He gave her a contact number for the station, made sure Poppy felt ok to cope and left.

Poppy sat down behind the counter trying to think what to do next. Suddenly Jason's name popped into her head. Without thinking she took his card from the drawer and dialed his number.

"Hello, Frobisher Renovations," came the cheery answer to the call. When he heard her voice he said, "Oh! Poppy how good to hear from you, I thought my card had blown away when I didn't hear from you."

"But Jason, I did call," said Poppy, "the same morning you left your card. You were quite rude and said it wasn't a good time to talk."

"It wasn't me Poppy, honestly. I was looking forward to hearing from you. Oh crap! – sorry for the language, but I lost or misplaced my phone for a day or two, there was some disturbance in my office and I thought it might have been stolen then I found it on my desk the next day and I was sure I'd looked there. I am generally so careful with my phone because it's the link to my business." There was silence for a moment. "Maybe someone did break in and was looking for something," he said slowly.

"Jason, the shop has been broken into. The door is smashed and I'm quite scared," she said, her voice trembling.

"I'll be there in ten minutes, don't move." The phone disconnected and ten minutes later the truck screeched to a halt and Jason strode inside.

Poppy burst into tears and Jason put his arms around her and held her tightly.

"You'll be ok, I'll fix the door, you put the kettle on. A builder can't function without his mug of tea." He grinned gave her a quick hug.

"Then we'll sit down and you can tell me all about it."

She immediately began to feel better, if a little embarrassed at having cried on his shoulder. Jason went out to fetch his tools from his truck and she put the kettle on to make tea.

The locks replaced, Poppy and Jason sat at the counter. "Now tell me all about it," he said, looking her in the eye.

She took a sip of tea. "You're going to find this hard to believe."

His eyes widened as she began to tell him what happened after he'd left the trunk a few days ago.

"Well I am not sure what to think," he said slowly. "I've never encountered any ghosts before, but I must admit that the house I am renovating has an interesting atmosphere, warm, as if the people who lived there were happy. I am wondering about that suspect break in and there have been some people hanging around who aren't connected with the developer who bought the property, so maybe we had better take this seriously and make some enquiries."

"Where do we start?" Again there was a faint smell of violets in the air and for some reason she said firmly, "I think the answer lies in the trunk. It's in the back - let's have a look."

"OK, we have to start somewhere. I don't have to be back at the house until the afternoon, when the developer is coming round to see how the renovations are going."

Jason effortlessly picked up the trunk and carried it out to the shop where there was more space. Lifting the lid, they admired the condition it was still in and Poppy thought it might have been new when the clothes were packed away. It was empty, then Poppy remembered the dance invitations and cards she had taken out of the trunk with the clothes and gramophone. They were still in the boot of her car. She had forgotten to take them out after the shock of seeing the shop had been broken in to. They both went out and took the clothes, gramophone and records into the shop and securely locked up again. Amongst the cards was an envelope addressed to Primrose and Archie.

My Darling Primrose and Archie
Your father and I are devastated at your deaths and I don't know if we will ever recover. I know you will never read this but I feel I want to write to you and tell of our plans.

We can't remain in the home where you grew up and where we were all so happy so are closing up the house and going to America. Your father has a cousin in business and suggested we join him in New York. We are going to try and make a life although without you both it will be so difficult.

We have written to Mr Pritchard of Prichard & Alsop, our Solicitor in London who will keep the papers and any information about where we are. With no cousins or remaining family in England the house will remain unsold in case we decide to return.

My darlings I hope you were happy on your last night and you weren't too frightened at the end.

Your broken-hearted loving Mama and Papa.

Poppy brushed a tear from her eye as she finished reading the letter. "I wonder if Pritchard & Alsop still exist, I'll have a look," said Jason. Opening the white pages for London he searched for Pritchard & Alsop and could hardly believe it when the name came up with contact details.

Putting on a record of the Charleston, Poppy said, "maybe this will help us think what to do next."

A cheerful voice came from the back of the shop. "Good idea darling, aren't you both doing well!" The floating figures of Jack and Primrose appeared behind the rack of their clothes. Jason gripped Poppy and gasped, "I wasn't sure if I believed in ghosts but I certainly do now."

"The mystery is almost solved, you clever things. I told you Poppy that young man of yours would help. Soon Jack and I can rest, join our families and friends, keep going." Blowing a kiss the spirits faded away leaving the usual violet fragrance in the air.

Jason called Pritchard & Alsop and asked to speak to the person in the office who dealt with old records. Shortly he was speaking with a young-sounding Charles Harper who asked if he could help.

"It is a bit of a mystery, but would you have any record of a family with the surname Kedgley who lived in Cheltenham in the 1920's and may have gone to the US after a family tragedy?" After a lot of questions back and forth, Charles said he would do some research and call back very soon.

Within an hour the phone rang and Charles sounded quite excited. "I've been talking with my grandfather who was a solicitor here a long time ago. He remembers the Kedgleys and was a friend of the family. He told me what had happened and said it was such a sad time. I found the file and think I should come along to see you and discuss the contents of the will and papers left behind."

Poppy and Jason said they were available whenever it suited and they made a time for tomorrow afternoon.

Jason went off to his meeting with the developer Mike Watson, and casually asked him how he acquired the property. It turned out that the house had been abandoned for so long and despite notices in papers no one had turned up, so he made an offer to the local authorities and was accepted. Shortly after he had had a visit from a group of people who wanted to buy the land, bulldoze the house and build a group of townhouses on the site. He liked the house and thought if it was renovated and the garden landscaped some family might like to buy it. The group who wanted to buy were being increasingly aggressive and even interrupting progress on some of his other projects.

"Please give me a couple of days Mike, before you sell. Maybe let them think you are thinking about it. I have got an idea," said Jason.

"OK Jason, you've got a week, but financially I can't take any more disruption. There is nothing I can report to the police but I am almost sure the group who wanted to buy the land and bulldoze the house are the ones behind the problems."

Later the next day Poppy and Jason sat in the Vintage Shop, speechless, as Charles Harper from the solicitor's office told them what happened after the tragedy of the fire and the deaths of Jack, Primrose and their friends. The Kedgley family had gone to America and in partnership with his cousin Mr Kedgley had made a fortune selling cars in New York and Chicago. They had another child and never returned to England, although they planned to take their son one day. They had never talked about Primrose and Jack to Brian, it was too painful.

Philip Kedgley had a massive heart attack one day in his office and died. His wife died shortly after, heartbroken. Brian their son grew up and continued his father's success in business in America but he didn't know about the property in England. He travelled to England soon after his parents' deaths, married a girl he met, and settled down in Kent. They had three children. Their son and hiswife had a daughter Poppy and one of their daughters had a son and two daughters one called Clare about the same age as Poppy. This information Charles had discovered after Jason's enquiring phone call a week ago.

"I think I have to do some more research into this Poppy, but it appears that you and your cousins are heirs to the property in question," said Charles. "I do love a good who dun' it! My grandfather will be delighted that there is a happy ending to the sad story of his friends. I'll go over all the paper work and lodge your family's claim on the property." He took contact details of the developer Mike Watson to let him know the family would be in touch about how to proceed with the development. Then Charles smiled, shook hands with the young couple and hurried back to the office.

Talking over everything they had learned Jack went back to tell Mike what had happened and that the solicitors would be in touch with him and they would put a stop to the harassment of the group who had been trying to intimidate him.

"What I don't understand," said Poppy, "is why that horrible man wanted to buy all the clothes from the trunk, and why he broke into your office."

"I think from what Charles said, the statute of limitations or some such legal jargon means that shortly the inheritance would have run out. You, Clare and other cousins would have missed out as too many years have passed."

"I'd better get back and tell Mike that the mystery has been solved. First, let's see if we can get Jack and Primrose back on the scene and see what they think," said Poppy.

Jack put on one of the jazz records and the wonderful music filled the shop. The scent of violets preceded Primrose and Jack's appearance.

"I knew you looked familiar Poppy, now I know why! How marvelous – I must be your great, great, something Aunt!" Primrose laughed. "I knew Jason would help you solve it all. Thank you darlings! Have a happy life."

Slowly the ghosts of Primrose and Jack faded for the last time but Poppy felt in her heart that they would be always be nearby, especially when they played their wonderful records.

THE END

HOT FEET

"Hot," murmured Frances as her caregiver put her feet into a basin of hot water.

"Oh! Sorry Mrs. B. I should have checked the water," Polly, a cheerful woman who came in every day to look after Frances after she had had her stroke, quickly lifted the basin away, dried her feet then massaged soothing cream into them.

Settled again in bed feeling warm and comfortable Frances tried to smile at Polly but managed only a grimace. Polly understood and patted her hand. "I'll just tidy up and look in again before I leave."

Polly picked up towels and linen to be washed then left the room humming to herself.

Frances began to doze and suddenly a vision appeared. It was her earliest memory. There were crowds of very tall people, her mother's skirts, brass band music, cheering and a peep of her Dada smiling at her from hundreds of other marching soldiers. She learned later that she and her mother had been waving off her Dad with the Australian Imperial Army as they marched to the ships for embarkation to sail to Gallipoli. Frances had taken off her shoes and socks and burned her feet on the sandstone pavement of Martin Place. "Hot feet," she had said to her mother as she was pulled through the crowds with her mother trying to catch a glimpse of her young husband she wouldn't see again for another three years.

"Ok, Mrs. B. everything is ship-shape in the kitchen, Phyllis will be home in a few hours and I'll see you in the morning." Polly patted the old lady's shoulder, straightened the duvet and left.

A familiar pain crept across Frances' chest and down her arm. She reached for her angina spray and waited for the pain to ease and tried not to hold her breath while the discomfort subsided.

Tears of frustration for the long-gone, busy full life she had led trickled down her face. She looked at the photographs her daughter Phyllis had placed within view; her parents, children and grandchildren, friends and family – school days, weddings, babies, graduations all marking special events. Her eyes searched along the shelf until they stopped at a small photo of a young man seated at a piano. Lenny, he had been smiling at her as she took the photo.

The years rolled back again and the music of Benny Goodman and Louis Armstrong echoed in her memory. She was 17 and at the local dance hall with her girlfriends. For some reason she had been full of excitement that day with the feeling that something wonderful was about to happen. She felt the world was at her feet and she could do and be anything she wanted. Laughing and jitterbugging with the girls and some of the young men she knew from the neighbourhood, Frances became aware of someone watching her. The Piano Player smiled, lifted his hand from the keyboard and gave her a little wave.

Soon after she felt a hand on her arm, and a voice said, "Can I have this dance? I'm on a break." She felt the excitement of the unknown run through her veins as she nodded her acceptance. "I'm Lenny, I've seen you here before and wanted to meet you and hoped you would spare me a dance." He smiled his heartbreaking smile and they danced together as if they already knew each other's steps. Too soon he had to go back on stage again.

"Wait for me when the evening finishes, I have to talk with you, please?" he gazed into her eyes and she answered, "Yes."

Frances told her friends not to wait for her as she would catch the last bus home. They weren't keen on leaving her, but she was determined. "I'll be OK, see you at church tomorrow morning."

She sat at a table near the stage and as it got later and the band still played she got a little nervous wondering if she would miss her bus.

It was nearly midnight when gathering up her coat and bag, Frances decided she had better run for the bus and she couldn't wait for Lenny any more. As she turned to go she felt a hand on her arm and heard a voice in her ear.

"Not leaving are you, Frankie?" said Lenny.

"I have to leave, if I miss the last bus I'll get in trouble," stammered Frances.

"I'll walk you home," said Lenny, "I want to see you again and get to know you." He picked up her coat and put it around her shoulders, took her hand and guided her out through the last of the dancing crowd.

It was a beautiful Sydney evening. A full moon hung low in the sky, a light breeze blew in from the harbour and the young couple gazed at each other knowing they were beginning something extraordinary. Lenny took her hand, tucked it into his elbow, gazed into her eyes and said, "Which way is home, Frankie?"

As they strolled along the waterfront they gazed in amazement at the rising Sydney Harbour Bridge and the two spans which had been joined that month. All too soon they reached Paddington where Frances lived.

"I have to go, I've never been out this late before, my Mum and Dad will be very angry if they are awake." She looked anxiously towards the house.

"I'll watch to see you are safely inside, wave to me from your window and then I'll go. When can we meet again? We are playing again next Saturday at the dance hall, you will be there won't you?" Lenny asked, holding on to her hand tightly.

"Yes if I can." He kissed her cheek and she ran quietly towards the back door which was generally left unlocked. Soon after, she leaned out of her bedroom window and blew Lenny a kiss.

"Sshh! Go to sleep," she whispered to her sister as she climbed into bed beside Maggie who had stirred as the blanket was pulled back.

The week crawled by, going to work and fielding questions from her friends about the piano player.

One evening when she arrived home from work her Dad was sitting on the veranda. He called, "Hey Frances, come and talk with your old Dad for a while."

"I'll just say hello to Mum. Shall I bring you a beer Dad?" asked his eldest daughter.

"Thanks Frances, you're a good girl," said her Dad lighting up another cigarette.

When she had come outside and poured her Dad's beer, they sat for a while looking out over the garden.

"Well Frances, when are you going to tell me about your young man?" asked her Dad, smiling while at the same time trying to look severe.

"What young man?" stalled Frances, trying to stop any further questions.

"The one who kept you out late last Saturday night, the one who watched while you got inside safely." He smiled, "I figured if he was that thoughtful, he might just be a considerate young man."

"You never said anything. I thought you were asleep," stuttered Frances.

"When my daughter is home safely then I go to sleep," her Dad answered. "I trust you but you can't always trust the young men around today."

Frances and her Dad talked until her Mum called them for dinner. "Before we go in Frances, I have something for you." He handed her a camera.

"It's called a Beaux Box Brownie, the latest thing. I did some work for a photographer today and he didn't have the cash to pay me so he offered this, he said it was brand new and took fantastic pictures. I thought you might like to have it, take pictures of the family and maybe your young man too." He smiled as his daughter threw her arms around his neck.

"Thanks Dad, I'll take some great photos! And the first will be of you – Smile!"

She pointed the little box and pressed the button.

The photo she had taken of Lenny the following Saturday at the dance was on her mantelpiece. Three months after she'd taken the picture, Lenny was dead. Coming home late from a wedding the band had played at, the van had crashed. Lenny and Joe the drummer died, Joe had been driving and fallen asleep at the wheel. Francis was heartbroken.

Seventy years later Frances lay in bed, dozing, pictures and memories running through her head. Working and laughing with her husband Pete and their three children. Her parents, brothers and sister. Cousins and friends. Half-forgotten memories jumped like a movie film that had jammed.

Then it all slowed down. Music drifted into the room and she saw herself at 17 in her favourite yellow dress, dancing with Lenny, her arms round his neck. She heard his voice reassuring, "It's all going to be ok Frankie." In the background she could see her Mum and Dad, there was a smell of frangipani just like the tree in their garden of the old house in Paddington. Pete and his family, there were her brothers and sister, who had died years ago, they were young again and smiling.

Frances relaxed and let the warm feeling of being loved wash over her. She closed her eyes and slipped into a deep sleep.

Phyllis arrived home an hour or so after her mother's heart had stopped. When she got over the shock she realized that her Mum was smiling, her face smooth and anxiety free. She couldn't understand why there was a smell of frangipani in the room.

WEEKEND IN RUSSELL

"I don't know how to thank you Maggie, you really are a dear good friend," said Rosalie as she got up to leave.

"Nonsense Rosalie, you are always there for me and everyone else. You've saved my sanity with tea and seeing the funny side of any problem over the years; now it is your turn. Off you go and enjoy that restful weekend before you get caught up in rush hour traffic!"

Rosalie gazed at the little dark head of her son Tim and the bright red hair of his friend Michael, both aged four, best friends completely engrossed in a complicated game which only four-year-old best friends could understand. She knew he would be happy and secure with Maggie, her husband Joe and their three children.

A quick hug all round and off she went with a few tears moistening her eyes. It was the first time she had left Tim for more than one night.

A weekend in Russell! Alone! Rosalie couldn't quite believe it. She loved Tim dearly but to have a few days without the constant demand on her attention, to relax and walk by herself would be wonderful. She had been so tired lately and had been getting tense and irritated with everyone at work and even her darling son. Maggie had planted the idea of a few days away and then dismissed all her objections until Rosalie finally agreed and here she was driving over the Auckland Harbour Bridge on her way north at last.

As she drove the memory of her last impromptu weekend away made her smile. Her husband Richard had arrived home early one Friday and said in that irrepressible way of his, "We're off on a magical mystery tour, pack the bags, Tim's nappies and let's go!"

An hour later with Tosca the dog and Charlie the cat farmed out to Maggie and Joe, the house was locked up, she was ushered laughing to the car where 18-month-old Tim was already strapped into his safety seat. They drove down to the beautiful Coromandel in the Bay of Plenty.

It had been a magical three days. They had made love under the stars, talked and laughed as they had before the arrival of Tim and a mortgage. At the little homestay holiday home where Tim had booked in at Cook's Beach, the owner's daughter had taken a shine to Tim and had played and looked after him all weekend. Richard and Rosalie returned to Auckland on Sunday refreshed and rejuvenated, promising each other they wouldn't let the pressure of everyday living stop them from putting aside some time each week to talk and catch up with each other on what they were thinking and feeling. Solve any worries before they became problems.

The memory of that weekend comforted Rosalie during the dark time after Richard's death. He'd been coming home from working late at the Computer Centre when a drunk driver lost control of his vehicle, veered across the motorway and smashed into Richard's car, killing him instantly. Another statistic, another victim of the culture of drinking and driving.

Two years later Rosalie still shivered when she thought of those awful months of coping and coming to terms that her best friend, her lover, husband and Tim's Daddy wouldn't be coming home.

The road north was fairly clear and she made good time, stopping for a rest and coffee in Whangarei before pressing on to Russell.

"Hello men," said Joe to Michael and Tim as he arrived home from work. After distributing hugs, swings and pats to children and dogs respectively, he planted a kiss on his wife's head and sat down at the kitchen bench to exchange news of the day.

"Rosie get away OK?" he asked Maggie.

Maggie smiled at her tall, red haired, skinny husband whom she loved dearly but who at times could drive her to distraction when he forgot time and got involved with one of his 'projects' in the garage and disappeared for hours at a time.

"Oh yes, after checking six times that Tim had everything he possibly might need for the weekend, plus a surprise for the boys if they get fretful, and a bottle of wine for us in case we got fretful! She is a dear." Maggie smiled and finished preparing dinner while Joe set the table.

"Did you tell her Phillip would be there?" asked Joe.

"Mmm! Well no, not exactly," said Maggie.

"That means no. Well I hope they get on better this time if they do meet. I won't forget that dinner party in a hurry. I don't know which one of them was in a worse temper. If one of them had said something was black the other would have sworn it was white."

"Well," said Maggie with spirit, "I think if they got to know each other they really would enjoy each other's company. It shouldn't be allowed, two good-looking, intelligent, kind people who have both lost someone they loved dearly, being alone. I know they would be good for each other. Anyway Philip is far too attractive; at least he is when he smiles – to be let loose on those calculating females in his office. Rosalie is just right for him, you'll see." All the same she was slightly apprehensive about their reaction if the 'accidental' meeting didn't work out.

"Philip is certainly taking a long time to get over Claire dumping him for Karl. Just because the Swiss gnome had bank accounts in five different countries, three houses and a yacht. I think Philip was obsessed with Claire - those types of female are too hot to handle," said Joe, giving his wife a cuddle. "I am so glad I have a wife who completely understands me." They were giggling when Josie their oldest child bounded in demanding dinner as she was 'starving.'

About an hour later Rosalie telephoned to say she had arrived safely and was settled into the Duke of Marlborough Hotel. She wasn't too tired and was just going to get something to eat. Maggie reassured her Tim was very happy and Joe was reading the children a bedtime story.

Next morning after a deep dreamless night's sleep, Rosalie woke without that awful tired feeling she had been experiencing these past few months. Going to the window she pulled back the curtains to let in a beautiful sunshine-filled morning. The Bay sparkled, yachts bobbed on the water and people strolled in shorts and tee shirts; it must be warm. Quickly she stepped into the shower, got dressed and hurried down for breakfast, eager to be on her way to explore the old township.

The dining room was about half full and from the accents she could pick out, there were American, Japanese and Europeans laughing and talking. She sat down and smiled at the person sitting at the next table, a young fair haired man, brown as a suntan lotion advertisement with sun-bleached hair. He said "Good Morning,

112

wonderful day," in a gentle Southern American accent.

Rosalie ordered her breakfast was soon finished and on her way. As she passed her American neighbour's table he said, "Have a nice day," and for once she was not irritated by the remark, it sounded as if he genuinely meant it and she had never heard the glib comment before.

Collecting her bag with sunglasses, jacket and book, off she went feeling really good, relaxed and slightly guilty as if she was playing truant from life. She strolled down to the wharf where boats, yachts and the ferry from Paihia across the Bay were tied up. Looking into the sparkling clear water, she was amazed to see hundreds of tiny and not so tiny fish darting around. Half a dozen small boys and girls sat with fishing lines dangling over the side and the squeals of delight from the young fishermen as they caught another fish brought a smile to her face.

"They are having as much fun catching their fish as the man who caught that 110 kilo swordfish on the weighting block did," said a deep voice a few yards away.

Rosalie looked up with astonishment at the tall figure leaning on the wharf railing. The voice seemed vaguely familiar.

"Philip Ashton. We met about two months ago at Maggie and Joe's," said the tall dark haired man. She couldn't see his eyes hidden behind sunglasses. He smiled and his face took on a completely different appearance. The closed-in, defensive look disappeared.

Mmmm! He is quite good looking after all, Maggie was right, said Rosalie to herself. Out loud she replied, "Oh! Yes Philip I remember. I am afraid I wasn't very good company that evening. Life had been rather stressful and Maggie thought I needed cheering up. I didn't contribute much sparkling conversation that evening." She smiled and held out her hand. She was unprepared for the tingling shock as a warm firm hand grasped hers. Putting on her sunglasses to hide her confusion, she asked. "And what are you doing here?"

"Well, I have been rather tense lately; barking at my poor secretary, working long hours and then fell victim to one of the viruses floating around and couldn't seem to shake it off. Joe recommended I come up here for some rest and recuperation. How about you?"

"Mm, something along the same lines as you, only Maggie recommended I come up here."

Both were silent for a moment, and then burst out laughing.

"Maggie's matchmaking." They said together smiling at each other.

"Do you mind?" he asked. "We could have some fun exploring together and I would enjoy your company, now that both of us have improved our tempers!"

"Not at all," said Rosalie, "I'm glad to have someone to talk to, as long as it isn't about the cost of living or how soon the statistics report will be completed! Russell certainly is a welcome change from Auckland."

They strolled off towards Pompalier House, built in 1841, tentatively talking at first, and then gradually relaxing. The beautiful old fashioned garden of the house, bees buzzing around the blossoms, heady perfume from the flowers, and a gentle breeze through the trees created a magical atmosphere where they strolled, sometimes talking, sometimes not.

In a hidden corner of the garden they both bent to smell a rose and gently bumped heads. Rosalie felt her cheeks blush as their eyes met and she felt a long forgotten churning in the pit of her stomach. She had difficulty steadying her pounding heart. Surely he must notice. To hide her confusion she turned away and pretended to look at the herb garden. It was so long since Richard had held and loved her, she missed his closeness and warmth. She took some deep breaths and, composed again, turned and smiled at Philip who was following her down the path.

They had a wonderful day exploring the township, looking at the oldest surviving church in New Zealand, built in 1836 complete with walls scarred from musket balls from one of the many skirmishes the early pioneers had to contend with. Arts and Crafts shops had sprung up in recent years run by people from all over the world who considered the rest of the world well lost for life in beautiful Russell in the Bay of Islands New Zealand.

After lunching on grilled fresh fish pulled from the water a few hours earlier accompanied by a wonderful light local Pinot Gris they found a quiet spot on the beach under a pohutukaka tree and talked and talked. Philip for the first time talked in depth of how Claire had hurt him. How much he had loved her and when he discovered she was cheating on him with a Swiss financier she had met while on a fashion shoot in Milan, he was devastated. Arriving home from a business trip to Sydney two years ago he found a letter propped up on the drinks trolley.

"It has been wonderful darling, but time to move on. Karl can offer so much more in Europe for my career – no hard feelings, Ciao, Claire."

I was devastated," said Philip. "I hadn't realized how vulnerable I was and vowed it would never happen again. I buried myself in my work." He looked closely at the slim pretty woman who sat listening sympathetically. She didn't offer platitudes, just squeezed his hand and he felt that she understood how lost he had felt.

"Do you know," he said in amazement, "that is the first time in two years I have talked about Claire without a knife twisting in my gut. I think I am cured, and I think I was obsessed by her rather than being in love," and he leaned over and brushed his lips lightly over Rosalie's cheek. She jumped as if burnt. Philip put his arm round her and said, "Don't worry, we'll take it slowly. Now tell me all about you. You have been listening to me for the last hour or so – it's your turn now."

Hesitatingly Rosalie began to talk of how she and Richard had met in Australia seven years ago when they were both on holiday. They had travelled around Australia and returned to New

Zealand to marry. Tim was born exactly nine months later and they were so happy, working hard on the tiny house they had bought, planning their lives until that fateful night when a drunk driver had wiped out all their plans and Richard's life.

She tried to explain her feelings of anger at the unfairness of it all; the drunk driver had escaped with a broken wrist and a fine. Richard had been going to see an Insurance Broker to arrange life insurance, the appointment was for the week following his death. It had broken her heart to have to go back to work and leave Tim in a day-care centre. Maggie had him two days a week, but she couldn't expect her friend to have him all the time. She had enough to do with Josie at school, Michael the same age as Tim and now nine-month-old Megan. As she talked tears began to flow and Philip was upset that she was so distressed.

"Don't worry," she sniffed, "I'm fine really, and I feel as if a plug has been pulled on my emotions, bottled up over the last two years. It's as if a stone has been lifted from my heart and all the sadness is drifting away. Thanks Philip for listening, I haven't been able to talk to anyone else like this, not even Maggie.

He leaned over and kissed her again, this time gently on the lips, they tasted salty from her tears. Holding each other tightly for a few minutes while catching their breath, each feltthe other's heart beating wildly.

"Come on," he said huskily, "I think it is time we got moving, the sun is going down. There is a great little restaurant on the waterfront, I'll try and get a table while you get changed." They walked back to the hotel. Philip kissed her forehead and held her tightly. "To think I nearly didn't come on this weekend break. What would I have done if our paths hadn't crossed again?" He gently pushed her towards the stairs.

Rosalie's heart sang as she ran upstairs, she stopped and looked back. Philip had just turned away and she stood and admired his body in well-fitting jeans and beautifully tailored casual shirt. He turned and caught her watching him and they grinned at each other. She blew a kiss and went to her room. She turned on the taps of the old fashioned deep bath and poured in two sachets of bubble bath. There was an hour and half to get ready; lovely, time to relax and think. As the fragrant water soothed her body Rosalie thought of the day. How different from the dinner party at Joe and Maggie's when they had been two stressed-out individuals and couldn't stand the sight of each other. She laughed and raised the glass of wine she had treated herself to from the mini bar, "Thanks Maggie!"

Just after 7.00pm she was dressed and walked down the stairs to the lobby of the hotel. Thank heavens she had brought her one good dress. Rosalie felt wonderful in it, a floaty rainbow of colours with matching scarf, she blessed the day she had bought it in a sale and put off paying the telephone bill for another week. Philip walked in looking elegant and handsome in beautifully tailored trousers and jacket. When he saw Rosalie walking down the stairs the smile that transformed his remote features broke out and he walked over took her hand and kissed her on the cheek.

"You are so beautiful!" he said, smiling. "I am the happiest man in Russell to be escorting you and have your company." They strolled out into the balmy evening, admiring glances following the attractive couple.

"The restaurant is an old converted colonial cottage and the food the best this side of Ponsonby I've been told," Philip said. "Our table won't be ready until eight – are you warm enough for a stroll along the wharf?"

Yes, thank you – I feel wonderful, the weather is amazing, arranged especially for us," Rosalie smiled.

Philip suddenly laughed and said, "Do you think Maggie arranged the weather too?" He pointed out over the bay towards the most glorious red-gold full moon which was rising above the horizon. Neither had seen one like it before. It seemed close enough to touch and the moonlight reflected on the water made a path across the gently lapping waves straight to where they were standing at the end of the wharf. They stood wrapped in the magic of the evening as music from the hotel, cafes and nearby moored yachts drifted along the beach.

Turning towards each other they both knew this was a moment in their lives they would never forget. Their kisses were no longer tentative and gentle but passionate, full of longing, exploring – they leaned for support on the wharf rail, he kissed the pulse in her throat and she twisted her fingers through his hair.

And so began the most romantic evening of Rosalie's life. She felt cherished and cared for, and they laughed and talked easily as if they had known each other forever. The waitress gave them special attention and the other diners looked with interest at the couple who were oblivious to anyone else, and smiled at the atmosphere which enveloped the lovers. At midnight they were the last people in the little restaurant. Philip had been right; the food was delicious accompanied by the perfect wine. Before they asked for the bill, the owner and his one waitress joined them with a special bottle of port which Harry kept for customers he felt deserved the best.

"You two have spread a little magic here tonight, you've earned a glass of this very good port, tell me what you think, or if you prefer, a brandy?"

The port was superb and finished off a perfect evening. Harry told them stories of his customers from all over the world who took some time out of life to recharge batteries in Russell. The men who owned islands in the Bay of Islands, European and American multi-millionaires who in their own words, owned a little piece of paradise. From time to time they appeared for a few weeks to recover from stresses of high pressure business, to relax, do a little fishing and escape from deadlines and demands on them.

They finally said good night to their host, promising to return, and walked slowly back to the hotel, a little heady with the wine, atmosphere and the evening. On one side of the path were little cottages, a museum, native trees and flowers, on the other the dark blue water edged with lacy white foam splashing gently on the sand.

At the door of the Duke of Marlborough Philip kissed her gently on her nose. "Off to bed, we've had an incredible day, get some sleep and I will pick you up after breakfast." He hugged her briefly. "If I stay here I'll ravish you on the steps of this staid and correct hotel." Patting her bottom he said, "Sleep well my darling, see you tomorrow after breakfast."

Rosalie ran upstairs, fumbled with her key in the lock and hurried to the window to see him disappear in the direction of his motel. As she prepared for bed, she guiltily remembered she had hardly thought of Tim all day, except when she was telling Philip about him. Still Maggie would phone if anything was wrong.

Contrary to what she thought Rosalie was soon asleep and just before she woke at dawn she dreamt of Richard. He was standing under a tree with sunlight behind him; he smiled his crooked smile that she loved and spoke.

"Goodbye Rosie my love, you are going to be fine now." The image faded until he disappeared. Rosalie woke with a start and with amazing clarity felt a chapter in her life was finished – a new one beginning.

From the window she saw the weather had deteriorated a little from yesterday, but it still was a wonderful day for soon she would see Philip. By 8 o'clock she was eating breakfast when her tanned American neighbour from yesterday appeared and asked if he could join her. Rosalie felt so happy she said, "Certainly, please do." He soon had her laughing at his wildly-exaggerated stories of life crewing on a yacht which so far had taken two years sailing round the world. He was staying at the Duke of Marlborough Hotel while waiting for his next crewing job.

Dave had dropped out of his father's business in Dallas Texas and didn't miss the high pressure business life at all. "Only thing missing is a lovely lady like you to share my hammock," he flirted, lifting her hand to his lips to plant a lingering kiss.

Just then Rosalie noticed Philip standing white-faced in the doorway of the dining room staring at them. Her head had been thrown back laughing at Dave's outrageous flirting.

Philip turned on his heel and stormed out.

Rosalie ran after him and caught up with him on the path leading away from the hotel.

"Philip, what's wrong?" she asked.

"I might have known, you can't trust any woman. Did you sleep with him last night, after you left me?" he snarled with a face like thunder.

"How dare you," she raged, almost in tears. "He is just a funny young man whose second nature is to flirt and if you are so untrusting I never want to see you again!"

Rosalie rushed off in the direction of the hotel and dashed up the stairs ignoring Dave who called after her.

She couldn't believe what had happened and distraught, threw a few things in a bag. Hearing footsteps on the stairs she rushed to her window, threw it open and stepped out onto the fire-escape then climbed down to the ground. She ran down the beach in the opposite direction to where she and Philip had so happily strolled yesterday.

Sobbing, she climbed over the rocks around the bays, not knowing where she was going, just to find somewhere to be alone and to try and make sense out of Philip's dreadful reaction to her talking to another man.

Walking and climbing over the rocks, her mind and emotions churning, she didn't notice the sky darkening. A storm was brewing and the tide was coming in. As the first heavy drops of rain started falling Rosalie looked up at the sky, missed her footing and slipped. Her right foot became caught firmly between two sharp rocks. The rain was pouring down and the sea, so beautiful and calm yesterday, looked grey and menacing. As she desperately tried to free her foot Rosalie felt the first splash of the sea as the tide crept nearer.

"Help, help! Oh! Please someone help me," she cried. There was no one to hear except the sea gulls crying above her. Strangely she remembered her Irish grandmother telling her sea gulls were the spirits of sailors who had drowned. Before she drifted into unconsciousness from the pain in her foot she wondered if her spirit would become a sea gull.

"Rosie, Rosie," she heard her name in the distance and then felt strong arms supporting her. She opened her eyes to find Philip, grim-faced, holding her tightly and Dave chipping frantically at the rocks which trapped her foot, trying to see under the water where she was caught.

"Philip," she began.

"Don't talk," he ordered, "just concentrate on helping us get you out of here." Frantically Dave wrenched her foot from the loosened rocks before the next wave crashed over them.

"The ankle bone looks broken, Phil," said Dave, "we'll have to carry her."

"Heavens," thought Rosalie, "Philip looks so angry I expect he doesn't want to have anything to do with me anymore." Emotional and in pain, tears slipped down her face. Philip paused in helping Dave move the rocks so they could get out of danger and kissed her fiercely saying, "Don't be frightened, we'll get you out." In spite of her fear, the pain in her foot and the fact she was sitting waist-high in water, her heart began to lighten.

"I expect this will make a great story, rescuing a silly damsel in distress, to entertain girls in different ports!" Rosalie said with a little smile to Dave trying to lighten the drama a little.

"Certainly will Princess," said the chirpy American. "OK Phil, we'd better try and get on our way, that foot looks pretty bad."

Philip caught her up and for a moment held her tightly in his strong arms, too emotional to move. "I was so afraid we wouldn't be able to get you free," he muttered against her hair.

"Come on you love birds, let's get going before we are all drowned!" Dave hurried them along, timing each rock climb when the waves had receded. Somehow between them and with Rosalie helping as much as she could, they clambered over the rocks towards Russell and safety.

Later that afternoon, Rosalie was tucked up in bed; the doctor had just left after strapping her ankle, ordering rest and no rock climbing in the near future! Philip put his head round the door. "Can I come in?" he asked.

Rosalie blushed, remembering him carrying her up the stairs, taking her wet clothes off and putting her in a hot bath, tenderly washing and drying her, trying not to bump the injured ankle. He'd tucked her up warmly in bed just as the local doctor arrived.

"Philip, please come in and tell me how you found me and why was Dave with you?"

Philip looked uncomfortable. "I'll never forgive myself for such a stupid reaction when I saw you and Dave together. When I saw him

128

kissing your hand I immediately saw Karl kissing Claire's hand the first time I caught them together – my mind just boiled over in a black rage. Will you ever forgive me?" he begged.

Rosalie held out her arms and twenty minutes later when they had kissed thoroughly he gathered he was forgiven.

A gentle knocking on the door brought them down to earth. Philip opened the door and Dave popped his head around. "Just had to see what the Doc said and if you are going to be OK, Princess."

Rosalie assured him she was much better.

"I can see that," he said slyly, grinning at Philip, causing her to blush again. "I shan't interrupt; you two obviously have lots to talk about. I've asked the desk to send up some hot soup, toast and a bottle of brandy."

"Thank you Dave, you have been wonderful. Thank you so much," said Rosalie sleepily. Feeling the warmth of the blankets and hearing the howling gale outside, she tried not to think what would have happened if the two men hadn't found her.

"Thanks Dave, I'll buy you a drink later when Rosalie has gone to sleep. You saved not only her life but mine as well."

Dave blew a kiss to Rosalie, grinned at Philip and went downstairs.

The soup, toast and brandy arrived, the waitress set up the table close to the bed and after making sure they had everything they needed closed the door gently behind her.

With a bowl of delicious chicken soup inside them, and a tot of brandy at hand, Philip began to tell Rosalie how they had found her. "Dave found me prowling around outside, and after he had given me his version of your breakfast together and told me not to be such a damn fool, you had disappeared. The porter told me he saw you climbing down the fire escape and going off in the direction of the rocks. When the weather started changing Dave said he would come with me to look for you. Thank God he did." He paused to kiss her again and then continued the story. "We set off round the rocks and with the changing weather and the tide coming in we were really worried. I was getting desperate when we couldn't find you, then we heard a faint cry. I wasn't sure if it was you or the seagulls, but someone must have been guiding us, another twenty minutes and it might have been too late."

Rosalie had a sudden mental picture of her dream of Richard.

"Precious girl," Philip said, "I know we haven't known each other very long if you count the days, but I feel we have known each other forever. Can you imagine spending your life with a sometimes hot-tempered idiot?" He looked fierce and tense again.

"Oh! Philip darling, what about Tim, are you really sure, I get quite stroppy myself from time to time, could you put up with me?" She gazed up at him from her pillows.

"I can't stand it anymore," growled Philip, "I'm coming in beside you."

He locked the door, pulled the heavy drapes, turned the lights down all but a gentle lamp alongside the bed, stripped off his clothes and slipped in beside her.

He put his arms around her and she lost her breath as she felt his hard body against hers. "Now my girl, if it wasn't for your ankle we'd be making mad passionate love, but as it is we'll have to make the best of it." He kissed her hard again. "I'm waiting for an answer; can you imagine spending the rest of your life with me, Tim and all the other children we are going to have?"

"I think I'd better say yes, although we might have to have a discussion on how many other children. But I can't remember when something felt so right, I feel as if I have come home."

Their lips met tenderly; sweetly they nuzzled each other's face and neck inhaling the scent of their skin. Philip caressed her body, feeling it come alive. "Lie still," he commanded softly, "I want to know you and for you to feel everything. Don't move, don't think, just feel."

Beginning with her eyelids he gently kissed and nibbled her body, slowly exploring, discovering her warmth and pushing her arms that reached hungrily for him away. "I told you to just feel, I love you so much my darling I want to show you how much."

Rosalie surrendered to the overwhelming rush of pounding blood, the incredible sureness of his hands on her body; his lips on her breast brought her to where she felt she was floating outside her body. "Please Philip, now," she begged, her arms strained his body closer and they were locked together at last fulfilling the hunger and desire which had been building between them over the past few days. The storm raged outside – an accompaniment to the passion overwhelming the lovers inside.

Next morning, drowsy with the drama of the day before and the wonderful release of pent-up emotion for them both, Rosalie lay with her head on Philip's shoulder while they made plans for travelling back to Auckland and their future together.

"Shall we play Maggie and Joe at their own game?" said Philip with a grin. "I'll phone and pretend their plan was a disaster."

When the phone rang Maggie and Joe were laughing at Michael and Tim who were playing Zoo Keepers and feeding building blocks through the bars of Megan's playpen. "Well," said Maggie, I suppose she does look like a tiger in her orange striped baby suit. Answer the phone will you honey?"

"Hello, Auckland Zoo," said Joe cheerfully into the phone.

"Joe, it's Philip," a sharp voice came down the telephone wire. Joe put his hand over the mouthpiece and hissed to Maggie, "it's Philip." Maggie quickly put her ear to the other side of the phone.

"Yes Philip, how has your weekend been…" began Joe.

Philip interrupted in a bad tempered tone. "What do you mean by not telling me your irritable neighbour was going to be up here? She has completely disrupted my restful weekend. I have a bone to pick with you and Maggie. I'll call in on the way home this evening."

"Oh! Righto Phil, see you later." Joe hung up with a groan. "He will be unbearable next week, that's torn it."

"Mmm! I don't know so much," said Maggie thoughtfully. "I'm sure I heard someone giggling in the background and I am certain I heard kissing noises! I wonder?"

THE END

FINDING MAUREEN

(A sequel to the story LEAVING DANNY which appeared in the first collection of TALES TO READ IN A HAMMOCK)

Sunlight filtering through the curtains of the spare bedroom woke Maureen. She felt a little disoriented for a moment waking in an unfamiliar bed. As the events of yesterday crept into her mind, she smiled and stretched. It was a very long time since she'd woken refreshed after a good night's sleep. She didn't feel anxious as usual, her mind ticking over all the things she had to do for her family.

Looking at the bedside clock she remembered her admonition to Danny and the children to be down for breakfast at nine o'clock. The house was quiet. Usually on a Saturday she would be knocking on Jessica and Bryan's doors reminding them of where they had to be that morning. Hesitating, the habits of years almost getting the better of her, Maureen decided she had better start as she meant to go on.

'Good Morning Danny,' said Maureen cheerfully, 'put the coffee on will you please?'

Danny was so surprised at being asked to do something he got up and began to prepare the coffee, opening several cupboards before he found everything. Bryan finished setting the table.

'Thanks Bryan,' said his Mum smiling, 'that looks good, just put the milk in a jug would you please? That looks better.'

'Shall I call Jess?' Bryan asked, as his sister hadn't appeared.

'Oh, I don't think so,' answered his Mum, 'I told her to be here at nine and breakfast is nearly ready. You and your Dad are here and I am sure she will make it too.'

Maureen mentally crossed her fingers as her daughter almost had to be dragged from her bed every morning.

Putting toast on the table along with a plate of pancakes and another of bacon, she sat down, not in her usual chair, closest to the stove where she could cater for more requests, but in a chair near the door where Jessica usually slouched with eyes glued to her cell phone.

Just as everyone had helped themselves and Danny had poured coffee, the door burst open and an angry Jessica stormed in still in her dressing gown.

'What's going on? Why didn't someone call me?' she demanded.

'Good morning Jessica,' answered her mother cheerfully, 'I told you last night breakfast would be ready at nine, your brother and father made it on time, I was sure you would too. Sit down and have some pancakes.'

Her stomach got the better of her temper and she sat down in the chair her mother usually sat in.

'What are you playing at, Maureen?' said Danny peremptorily, trying to assert his authority and feeling uneasy at the same time.

'Nice breakfast thanks Mum,' said Bryan crunching on more bacon. He hadn't for a long time thanked his Mum for anything she had done.

'Why thank you Bryan,' she said brightly, resisting the temptation to fuss over him. 'I appreciate you saying so.'

'So what's going on Maureen, what's all this about, you expect us to thank you for everything now?' Danny blustered as he took the last pieces of bacon and toast.

Maureen ignored him and looked at her husband and children sitting round the table, trying to remember when anyone had exchanged a word other than demanding something.

'Have you all finished? I have something to say to you all, I want you to think about it and decide what you want from me and our lives together.'

'I'm busy,' said Danny getting up from the table, thinking how soon he could be on the first tee at the golf club.

'No, you're not Danny, your golf morning can wait,' said Maureen quietly with a hint of steel behind her mild comment.

Surprised, Danny sat down. Jessica had also stood up, leaving her dishes as always, and was walking out the door.

'Sit down Jessica.' The same steely tone of voice made her daughter quickly retake her seat.

Maureen looked at the three figures round the table. She wondered if they were going to listen to what she had to say and if it would make any difference. Mentally shaking herself she looked at them all then spoke softly.

'My life changed yesterday. The bus I was travelling home in, carrying food I had shopped for during my lunch break for your dinner, almost had an accident. Fortunately it was avoided and no one was hurt. But I was shaken and it also shook me out of the apathetic life I've been living. I got off the bus, went into a pub nearby and thought about what would have happened if I had been killed or ended up in hospital. At first I wondered how you all would manage without me then I thought *what about me*? Was that my life? I realised how unhappy, how unloved, how uncared for I felt and that I didn't want to live that life any more. We have several options. Life can carry on for us all but I will no longer be at your beck and call. Either the four of us work together to build a good future for us, equally contributing to our lives or we live separately. Maybe in this house, until Jess and Bryan decide what they are going to do with their lives after they finish school. If we don't find a resolution then the other option for me will be to make a life for myself.

'For the last four years or so since I have been working in the city, this household hasn't been functioning as a family. I've been expected to do everything, provide cash for the extracurricular activities, all the extras to make life comfortable, plus keep the house going, do the shopping, cleaning, cooking, everything. You've come and gone as if this was a hotel with benefits,' she looked at Danny, who dropped his eyes. 'I've written out a fair division of the chores, shopping, cleaning. It may take some time to get used to it but if we work together it will get easier. In fact life may begin to be fun again.'

No one spoke. Maureen continued. 'I have thought about how I have been part of this family but feeling as if I didn't exist except to provide everything you need. I am going to make a proposal, I've written it all down, when I've finished I'll give you all a copy, then I am going out to have coffee with a friend and do some shopping, no not grocery shopping, something for me. I'll be back later and then we can talk some more.'

Maureen got up and left the table pushed her chair in and took her dirty dishes to the sink, rinsed them and put them in the dishwasher. 'I'll be back at one and I hope you all will have discussed what I've said and read my suggestions as to how everyone can contribute. I am open to ideas if you think you can improve on what I've said. We can talk about it later. See you this afternoon.'

She walked quickly out and closed the door. Leaning against the wall she took a deep breath and realised she was trembling with a little bit of apprehension and a bit of exhilaration at what she had done. She wasn't sure if when she returned, they would all be out and breakfast dishes still on the table. Ah! Well she'd face that when she came to it.

Maureen grabbed her bag and rushed out of the front door. It was a lovely morning so she walked the twenty minutes into the village and went into *Robin's Nest*, a local café with excellent coffee and even better food. Gillian was waiting for her with a big smile.

'How did you escape without being guilt tripped?' she asked her old friend. Maureen sat down took a gulp of the coffee Gillian had ordered for her and began to feel worried about what was going on at home. 'Cut it out,' said Gillian, 'I know that look, it is about time those kids and Danny appreciated you and pulled their weight around the house. I've got my lot on a tight leash.'

Maureen sighed, 'No you don't, they all adore you Gill, and most of all they appreciate you.'

'Look love,' said Gillian handing Maureen a paper napkin to wipe her eyes. 'I just expect them to help. I'm not a martyr, I ask them to do something without a question in my voice, just happily asking and expecting them to set the table, hang up the washing, put the washing in the machine, whatever. Then I thank them profusely saying quietly to each one, "*I just don't know how I would manage without you.*" They all think they are the glue that keeps the house running.'

The two women laughed and finished their coffee. Maureen quickly told her old friend what she had said to Danny and the kids and how she wasn't sure what she would find when she returned.

'Well done,' said Gillian when Maureen had finished. 'Now it is time for a bit of retail therapy and everything we're looking for is all for you.'

Gillian dropped Maureen off after a lovely morning window shopping, laughing and talking about going to yoga classes and maybe joining that book club they had talked about for years.

'Good luck,' Gill smiled at Maureen. 'If it is all a disaster inside, give me a call and I'll pick you up.'

'Thanks Gill, you are a good friend – with you and the memory of that guy taking a risk on his bicycle, I've been given a nudge to make some good changes.'

With a wave she took her key out and opened the door.

The house was quiet. No loud music from the kids' bedrooms. No TV with a sports programme blaring. Maureen felt her heart sink. It looked as if everything she had said had been ignored just like she had been.

She walked into the kitchen. Well, the table had been cleared. Her notes were still on the table, she didn't know if they had read them or not. The dishes had been put in the dish washer – amazing, but it hadn't been turned on. She grinned to herself. It was a start.

Before she could switch it on she heard Danny's car pull up outside. The door from the garage opened and Maureen heard a sound she hadn't heard for a long time, the kids and Danny talking and laughing together.

'Oh! You're back. We hoped we'd be back before you,' said Danny. They came in carrying bags of groceries. 'We found your shopping list and thought we'd do it together.' Danny sounded a bit unsure of Maureen's reaction. She was speechless.

'We got everything on the list Mum,' said Bryan proudly, 'and Dad got some extras and we are going to cook dinner tonight. Jess chose what to get.'

Maureen smiled broadly. 'Well I don't know what to say except, I'm very pleased.'

Danny said, 'We've talked about everything you said and realised that we've been very selfish, we do want to talk about it and see how we can turn things around. We don't want you to leave us, and you do know it will take a while for us to shake off our selfish ways, but we will try.' He sat down at the kitchen table looking anxiously at Maureen.

'I'll make some tea and we have some yummy biscuits,' said Jess, 'I'm sorry Mum, I've been such a cow, I'll try harder.

'Me too,' said Brian. 'Not that I've been a cow like Jess, but maybe a bit thoughtless.'

'Don't call me a cow,' began Jessica, her voice raised. 'Oops sorry, it will take a bit of time.' She grinned.

'One step at a time,' said Maureen with a relieved smile. 'I've allowed you to treat me badly by not speaking up sooner, but I was just so tired and depressed. Now things are going to change for the better and I think we need to begin by communicating and telling each other how we feel, being less selfish and considering everyone's feelings. We've made a start.'

Maureen began to reach for the kettle to plug it in and make tea, then she drew her hand back, smiled at Danny and the children and sat down. Between the three of them tea and biscuits were soon on the table, Bryan put the milk in a jug, and they began to talk over each other as they all tried beginning the process of returning to the family they once were.

THERE'S A COFFIN IN THE LOUNGE

Frank and Jenny with their three boys arrived in Mangere Bridge after travelling up from Wellington, stopping for a night here and there at places which took their interest. It had been a fun 'time out' for the family after the frenetic few weeks preparing to leave their home and begin a new life in Auckland. They were all excited about the new chapter in their lives and both Frank and Jenny had family just outside Auckland. An engineering job had been offered to Frank with Water Care in Mangere, helping with the major upgrade in the area and the likelihood of the job continuing after his contract was completed. Jenny and Frank had checked out all the information they could about the area and were pleased that Mangere Bridge appeared to be a good community with excellent schools and kindergarten for their youngest. There was Ambury Park Farm nearby, where the family could visit at the weekends and Manukau Harbour foreshore to walk along.

Jenny had also contacted local real estate agents to find a home to rent, and they'd found what they believed to be the ideal house. Checking it out on the agent's website they could see the house was elevated and had a lovely view over the farm and sea. It nestled at the foot of an extinct volcano called Mangere Mountain. Perfect, Jenny and Frank thought.

Until they arrived.

Their three young sons raced around the garden, happy to have some exercise after their long journey. The sun was setting and there was a wintery chill in the air when Jenny opened the door to the rental home in Mangere Bridge. The electricity wasn't on so she felt her way through the house. She shivered as she heard creaking noises at the back of the house and at the end of her vision she thought she saw something moving. A tapping noise from the back of the house made her heart beat faster. Pushing the door to the lounge open she suppressed a scream and ran outside.

'Frank, Frank, there's a coffin in the lounge!' Jenny's sibilant whisper was several octaves higher than her normal voice.

'A WHAT!' Frank whispered back incredulously, 'Is there a body in it?'

'Didn't look,' Jenny's voice trembled. 'I'll try and reach the letting agent. You'd better take the boys, find a takeaway and buy fish and chips for supper. I'll text when it's ok to come back.'

'Are you sure,' said Frank, 'will you be ok? I don't like to leave you.'

'I'll be fine, it was the initial shock. I don't want the boys to see it; there must be a logical explanation. I'll phone the agency and get it sorted, don't worry.'

Frank pulled his wife into a tight hug, gave her a torch from the car, bundled his protesting sons back into their car seats before driving off in the direction of the village.

Jenny was alone with the coffin.

Despite ringing all the rental agent's numbers, there was no answer. She left messages and was getting increasingly frightened.

She was getting desperate. There didn't seem to be any lights on in the houses nearby and the whole neighbourhood seemed dark and isolated. She didn't want the boys to see the coffin when they came home or they would have nightmares. What could she do?

Taking a deep breath and offering up a little prayer, she went inside again, using the torch Frank had given her. The house seemed to have acquired a life of its own. The torch threw shadows that made her jump. Her imagination went into overdrive, was that creaking a rocking chair in the next room? Was someone tapping at the window? *Oh! She thought please let the agent call back.*

Back in the lounge she took another look at the coffin. It was resting on four table chairs and covered in paintings. Looking closer she saw the moon and stars, bright tropical flowers, rainbows and birds. She had never seen a coffin like that in her life, not that she had seen many. Her Nana and Granddad who had died a few years ago, and a school friend who had been killed on an adventure trip to the South Island, were the only people she had seen in their plain ordinary coffins.

Jenny steeled herself and reached out to touch the lid.

It moved. She jumped back in fright. When her heart had stopped threatening to leap out of her chest, she realized the lid must be loose.

Lifting it carefully she peered inside. To her relief, it was empty. OK, she said to herself, it's just an empty coffin I need to get rid of it somehow before Frank and the boys come back.

She slammed the lounge door in anger. The agent had promised to have the electricity connected, switch on the hot water and have the house professionally cleaned before they arrived. It was very quiet with Frank and the boys gone; and there were still no lights on in nearby houses. Trying the agent, the phone again went to voicemail, she left another increasingly agitated message and waited for a call back.

Her cell phone beeped. A message from Frank, *'any luck?'*

Jenny called him.

'Frank, I can't think of what to do next! I haven't heard from the agent, and there's no electricity, but at least there isn't a body in the coffin.'

'Don't worry pet, I'm on my way back, I think I have a solution,' said her husband reassuringly. 'Thank goodness the coffin is empty.'

The three boys, tired after their long journey and full of fish 'n' chips, dozed in the back of the car. Frank put his arms around his wife.

'I phoned my boss and he suggested we lock up and stay at the Jet Park Hotel nearby, and we can get in touch with the agent in the morning. Things will look better then and I am going to insist the agent takes care of the hotel bill. Now I want to see the extra unexpected piece of furniture in the lounge.'

Taking the key and torch from Jenny he opened the front door and they went into the lounge. Opening the lid he confirmed it was indeed empty with no need to call the police. Frank and Jenny hurried outside, locked the door and jumped into the car.

Looking at each other they nervously began to laugh, 'I'm sure there must be a logical explanation – at least we hope there is. Now we need think about getting the boys into bed.' Frank started the car.

A little voice came sleepily from the back of the car. What's happening Dad?' asked Joe their eldest son. 'We're not going back to Wellington are we? I'm tired.'

'Don't worry Joe,' said his Mum soothingly, 'we're staying in a hotel tonight, you will soon have a nice bath and hop into a warm comfy bed.'

Frank was about to drive off when Jenny grabbed his arm, pointing to the bush at the back of the house.

A series of lights were coming through the trees.

Winding the windows down, they heard what seemed to be tuneless singing. In the darkness with only intermittent torch light they could make out a group of people approaching the house.

Frank turned the car facing the house and put the car lights onto high beam.

Despite Jenny begging him to stay in the car, Frank got out, locked the car and walked quickly towards the people who by this time were at the front of the house.

'What do you think you are doing?' he said angrily. 'I've just rented this house for my family. You're trespassing.' He could see a rag tag group of people dressed like hippies, one with a guitar slung over his back.

A tall woman at front smiled dreamily and spoke. 'Greetings, I've just come to collect something I've left behind. I used to rent the house but have moved on.'

'It wouldn't happen to be a coffin would it?' queried Frank. 'If it is, come back in the morning

152

when I have the agent here, no doubt she will have something to say to you. Now I'd like you to clear off, I have paid the rent, it's my home.'

He stood his ground until the group of men and women turned and trailed off into the bush.

Next morning after a good night's sleep in the hotel the family had breakfast, and while Jenny and the boys packed up, Frank went to reception to check out. While he was there he asked if they could direct him to the real estate agent's office in the village.

'You're in luck,' said the smiling girl behind the desk. 'Jackie from their office has just arrived. Hey Jackie, there's someone over here who would like to talk with you.'

A young woman came over to the desk and was introduced to Frank.

'Hello Frank, what can I do for you?' she smiled winningly at him.

'Did you check your phone messages last night?'

'Oh, goodness, I forgot my phone, left it here last night and I've just picked it up. I haven't got round to clearing the messages. She laughed nervously and picked up her phone.

Frank sat back in his chair. 'Well, I suggest you listen to the ones my wife left last night, when we arrived at the house you rented to us.

As Jackie listened to her cell-phone messages her eyes widened, her face paled under the layer of make-up, and her hand went to her mouth. 'I'm so sorry,' she stammered, 'I'll get it sorted.'

Frank spoke quietly, but firmly. 'We expect you will; and pay for our night in the hotel. I'll collect the family and meet you at the house shortly.'

Twenty minutes later Frank and family arrived at the house the same time as Jackie. She began apologizing profusely as she stepped out of her car. Frank had already warned Jenny not to be too forgiving, she was a kind girl and didn't like to make a fuss. As they walked up the drive, the boys already racing round to the back of the garden where there were trees to climb. Frank and Jenny began to tell Jackie about the group of people who had appeared at the house last night; and there they were - the assorted group of people, brightly dressed, lounging on the veranda. A bearded man was playing the guitar gently.

Jackie recognized one of the figures sitting cross legged on the veranda, who was singing softly to herself.

'You're Marta, aren't you? You used to live here,' said Jackie accusingly, 'Did you leave anything in the lounge when you left?' her voice rose.

'Peace be upon us all,' the tall wild haired woman rose and raised her hands in greeting. 'Yes I've been looking for my latest work of art, I couldn't remember where I left it,' she answered dreamily. 'Then I remembered it was still here in the house. An eco-coffin for people who want to be buried in natural material, earth to earth. I was wondering where I left it.' She beamed at how clever she was.

Jenny held Frank back before he told 'the hippy' how much apprehension she'd caused them last night. They walked away and left Jackie to speak with the 'Earth Goddess.'

It turned out that Marta, a celebrant for eco funerals and decorated caskets to order, was expecting the family who had bought the coffin for their son who had died in an accident. She had left the house setting up a new home out West, leaving one of the other members of her communal 'family' to take care of delivering the coffin. She apologized for the upset she had caused and offered a gift of a necklace she had carved and decorated. While Jenny occupied the boys in the back garden, Marta and her entourage picked up the coffin, loaded it into a brightly painted old VW and drove off.

Frank and Jenny were left to move into their new home.

'I called in to the Mangere Bridge Library,' said Jenny a few days later, 'and applied for library cards for the boys and me. I saw they have a Writers Group there. I expect they don't need any more members but I might write the story about 'A Coffin in the Lounge,' and see what they think.'

A BODY IN THE WOODS

'Don't touch it!'

'I have to, it might still be breathing.'

'It looks gross.'

'We can't leave the body lying there, we need to call someone.'

'No, we don't, if we walk past and pretend we haven't seen anything, no one will know.'

'We'll know.'

'Don't be such a pain, let's go, I'm afraid, if it isn't dead, it might *get* us.'

'What if it was someone we know? If it happened to us, you'd want someone to help, wouldn't you?'

'But I'm frightened.'

'OK you stay back and I'll touch the neck and see if I feel a pulse.'

'Be careful!'

'I can't feel anything, the skin is cold, maybe we'd better call the police.'

'But we'll get in trouble.'

'No we won't, we'll tell them we were just walking.'

'They will want to know why we were here so late at night.'

'We were just going for a walk, nothing wrong with that.'

'But it's really late, they'll say we shouldn't be here.'

'Look I'm going to call the police. We can't just walk by and do nothing.'

'Oh! Please don't, my dad will kill me if he knows that we were out so late, he thinks I'm in bed.'

'Stop thinking about yourself for a minute, what about that poor bloke laying there. The medics might be able to help him, what if he isn't dead?'

'Wait a minute, wait a minute, let me think, maybe if I go home and you call the police, then my dad wouldn't know.'

'Then what would the police say to me, out here alone and reporting a body? They would suspect me right away. We're each other's alibi.'

'I don't want to be an alibi. What's an alibi? I'm still scared.'

'Well I'm not exactly thrilled at us almost lying on a dead body.'

'DON'T say that, I'll really get in trouble, we'll say we were just walking.'

'Right, lend me your phone. I don't think I've any credit left.'

'I don't want you using my phone to report a body.

'Don't be stupid, your phone won't know the difference between you gassing with your mates and calling the police.'

'Alright be quick and don't talk too long, I don't want all my credit used.'

'Are you crazy? We are reporting what may be a crime, never mind the credit on your phone!'

'OH! Do you really think it is a murder? That's quite exciting.'

'Not for that poor bloke laying there, give us your cell-phone.'

'Mm, I might just call the police myself, I could be in the paper, *"Girl reports body in the woods."* I might get famous and be interviewed.'

'I don't believe you. One minute you don't want to know then you are fantasizing about your name in headlines.'

'Well you read about papers paying heaps of money for an exclusive.'

'I've had enough of this, give me your phone or I might be reporting two bodies.'

'OK, don't shout, hurry up I'm getting cold.'

'Police please, I want to report a body in the woods – oh, it's gone!'

'Good thing I wasn't dead. By the time you two made up your mind to get help I could have fossilized.'

A NEW YORK CHRISTMAS

Sarah completed the final proof read, edit, grammar and spell check then with smile and a sigh of relief typed *The End*!

She sat back in her chair and waited while her manuscript sped off through the magic of modern communication to her literary editor.

This was her eighth novel with the most unlikely hero, Detective Kev. Cavanagh. He had a limp from a botched broken leg repair, receding hair line and a scowl that could break rocks. She had sent her first attempt to at least ten publishers before finally being accepted. The popularity of the quirky stories grabbed the reading fans of detective novels and the next book was always eagerly awaited.

Sarah had decided after her latest book was completed she was going to New York for

Christmas. The romantic in her had always wanted to visit Times Square, admire the famous annual Christmas tree, watch the skaters, visit the beautifully decorated stores, and see as many shows on Broadway as she could. She had one day of book signing and meeting the staff at her U.S. publishers, but that was after she had had a week of relaxing and looking around all the places she had dreamed of seeing.

Louise, the brilliant contact at her literary agent's office, had efficiently booked a lovely boutique hotel, organized tickets to shows and for someone from their New York Office to meet her the morning after Sarah arrived. He would call to introduce himself and would be available to escort her around the well-known tourist attractions or whenever she needed company.

Touching down at Kennedy Airport, she collected her luggage and was quickly through Business Class checkout. A tall man with her name on a card was waiting in arrivals. He picked up her case, gave her that warm American welcome then ushered her into the biggest limousine Sarah had ever seen. Sinking back into the warmth and comfort Sarah enjoyed the drive even though they were held up by congested Christmas traffic. The driver pointed out some places of interest on the way before they finally arrived at the lovely hotel in the centre of New York. She received .a warm welcome from the reception staff, including being asked to autograph her latest book. Sarah still got a kick out of being asked to sign one of her books. Soon she was settling into her beautiful suite, with separate bedroom, a sitting room with desk and comfortable furniture, and the most mind bogglingly fabulous bathroom she had ever seen. It had piles of thick soft towels, a huge shower room, and a big spa bath, with a television angled above. In her years of struggling she had never imagined enjoying luxury like this.

I could spend my whole holiday in here she thought, and ran water into the spa bath, pouring in beautiful soothing bath oils to relax the travel aches out of her bones.

The suite was filled with flowers, a bottle of champagne and huge basket of fruit on the table. Pouring a glass of champagne, she sank into the bath, murmuring with satisfaction *I deserve this*. Then the phone rang. After muttering in irritation she realized there was an extension by the bath so lay back and said, 'Hello, famous novelist speaking,' there was silence for a moment, and then an amused voice said, 'Joe, escort of famous novelist speaking.'

'Erm, sorry,' Sarah spluttered. 'I've just arrived and I'm relaxing in the bath, enjoying this beautiful suite and really thinking I might spend my whole holiday here.'

'Well I am sorry to hear that as I have some very interesting places and things to show you in New York that I'm hoping you would enjoy.'

Sarah laughed, 'After a good night's sleep I am sure I'll be ready for whatever has been planned.'

'OK,' said the cheerful voice. 'Shall we meet in the lobby after breakfast and then go over what we thought you might enjoy? If there is anything you want to change it's no problem.'

'Thank you, I look forward to meeting you,' said Sarah, slipping further down into the bubbles. He had hung up before she realized that she didn't know how she'd recognize him.

After a good night's sleep wrapped in the impossibly soft warm bed, breakfast was delivered to her room, and by nine o'clock, she was ready for New York.

It was snowing outside so she dressed warmly, picked up her beautiful new coat and bag with credit cards, and then went happily down to the lobby. She was about to go to the desk to enquire if anyone had called for her when she saw a slightly rumpled man standing by a desk reading the paper. With a start she thought she recognized him. He looked up as he realized he was being watched, and smiled.

'You must be Sarah,' he said. 'I recognise you from the photo on your books.'

'Hello,' stuttered Sarah. As she gazed in amazement at Joe, she thought she was looking at Kev Cavanaugh – slightly receding hairline, and as he walked forward she noticed he had a slight limp, but his face was without the scowl. Watching as he walked towards her she realized that her imagination had played tricks. He was much better looking than Kev. Cavanaugh.

'Would you like a coffee here and you can tell me what you'd like to see? I believe this is your first visit to New York? I'll tell you what we thought you might like to see and experience, what shows we have booked, and some great places to eat. How does that sound?'

'It sounds perfect thanks Joe,' answered Sarah, 'and maybe you might show me some of the real New York as well as the famous must-see places.'

Joe grinned back at her and said, 'by the time we've seen it all you won't want to leave. The Big Apple will have captured your heart and you will be a real New Yorker.'

Her heart gave a little flutter, as she realized that she was going to enjoy being shown New York by this rather interesting man. He wasn't like Detective Kev. Cavanagh at all.

SOUNDS

Her life as she knew it ended with a cacophony of sounds.

A gurgling sound came from her mother's throat as she lay on the floor. Josie looked with detached interest as she heard in the background, sirens, lots of sirens. I wonder where they are going, she thought. In the doorway she heard a whimpering sound and turned to see her aunt clutching her cell phone with crackling sounds coming from it.

The evening had begun as had so many others. Her parents, sister, brother and Josie, sitting in the lounge before dinner catching up with the day. The room filled with everyone's self-important noisy voices, giving their opinion, talking about what they had done and achieved in the day. As usual nobody noticed Josie sitting in the corner behind a book. Her day wasn't spoken of or opinion sought. That day something important had happened, Josie had been offered a job. Several times she had tried to speak but the sound of her voice was drowned out by Serena's or Michael's tales of who had said what to them or where they were planning to go on holiday. Not even mother or father heard her voice. She remembered from her childhood the times her brother and sister took the limelight at family parties; good looking, confident, and her small dark quiet person sitting in the corner. Her grandmother's voice still echoed in her head.

'What a funny little thing, where did she come from? She is like no one else in the family,' then her tinkling little laugh.

Suddenly Josie heard screaming – and was shocked to realize it was her.

'Listen to me…I'm here in the room too…I have something to say, why will nobody hear what I have to say?'

For a few moments there wasn't a sound in the room until a sickening crack was heard as Josie picked up her grandfather's old blackthorn walking stick. Then struck first her mother, then her father, brother and finally her sister, everyone in the room in turn, as they gazed at her in stunned horror. Blessed silence for a moment after each thwack was heard, then grunting and a thump as the bodies slipped onto the floor.

Josie hadn't heard the sound of her aunt's cheery voice, 'It's only me,' as she let herself in and stopped at the door of the lounge.

It was a few seconds before her mind took in the scene in the room, then she'd gasped in disbelief. The next sound was her dialling the emergency services.

Over the years as Josie again sat quietly, this time in a secure unit, she went over the sounds in sequence, as they played over in her head what had happened the day she had got a job and was finally going to leave home and be heard.

Loud voices, screaming, crack, crack, crack, grunting, thumping, whimpering, dialing, sirens, and her little voice saying. 'I only wanted to be heard, someone to listen to me.' Then the last sound of the day a cell door slamming and a key turning in the lock.

THE CURIOUS CASE OF THE POISIONOUS POT PLANT

'Do you really have to make that noise right now?' Dr. Arnold Price snapped sharply at his assistant who was clicking his pen over and over while staring at his notes. The Forensic Pathologist and team were painstakingly searching through scientific data.

This murder was fascinating and frustrating. Dr. Price was a perfectionist and prided himself on being the most meticulous and accurate pathologist in his field. But he was stumped. He had never seen results like this before and all research had drawn a blank.

The body of a young man had been brought in a week earlier. After lying undiscovered for several weeks in unseasonably warm weather, decomposition had been advanced. There were no signs of blunt force trauma, no bullet wounds, no drug or alcohol overdose. Finally, after several fifteen-hour days, Steve, Dr. Price's assistant who was once again going over toxin reports; found a small anomaly. A tiny part of the fingers and arms showed deep seated inflamed deterioration which had been difficult to spot due to the advanced decay of the body.

Grateful to have something new to check, the men bent over their microscopes with renewed energy.

In the meantime the Detective Inspector in charge of the case had discovered the name of the young man, Hugh Beachy. His team was following up sketchy information about where he came from and who knew him. Sergeant Barbara Anderson was once again talking with neighbours of the basement flat where Hugh had lived for the last year.

An elderly lady opened the door two houses away, it had been checked twice before but there had been no answer. The white haired woman with intelligent eyes carefully looked at Barbara's war-ant card, at her photograph then her face. Satisfied, she opened the door wider.

'Come in dear,' she said with a smile. 'Would you like a cup of tea?'

'Yes please, Mrs. Hardy isn't it?' Sergeant Anderson asked with a smile. She thought she would get more information out of this bright woman if they were sitting chatting rather than it appearing to be an interview.

'Yes that's right, I'm Brenda Hardy. It's about that young man who died isn't it?' She bustled about opening cupboards, taking out cups, saucers and plates then a tin with home-made biscuits, setting them out while she waited for the kettle to boil.

'Sorry I haven't been around, but I had to go and look after my sister, she had a fall and was out of action for a few weeks, she's fine now and I came home yesterday. I read about Hugh's death in the paper. How can I help?'

Keeping her voice calm Barbara felt that she might at last be getting some answers about the mystery of Hugh Beachy's mysterious death.

'Did you know Hugh Beachy at all, Mrs. Hardy?' asked Barbara casually while her pulse beat a little faster as she waited for an answer.

'Why yes of course, he was a nice young man, quiet but ever so interested in gardening and plants. He took care of my garden for me. He told me he had wanted to study horticulture and he always dreamed about travelling to South

America. Travel to the rain forest and see for himself the plant life there. We had such interesting talks.' Mrs. Hardy paused to pour out a cup of tea for them both. 'Funnily enough, my late husband was interested in plants, especially rare species, and we often spent weekends when he retired visiting unusual gardens and Heritage Homes. He died a year ago and I do miss our little trips. In fact I had suggested to Hugh, for my birthday, we might have a trip to the country home with spectacular gardens. It has an area specializing in rare plants from all over the world. He was looking forward to the trip.'

Sergeant Anderson finished her tea and then casually asked, 'Did Hugh keep any of his tools, compost or plants in your garden Mrs. Hardy?'

'Why yes, I let him work in Arthur's shed in the back garden, I haven't been in there since I got back from my sister's.'

'Do you think I could have a look?' asked Barbara, wondering if she should call the boss first, then deciding to check it out herself.

'Of course, I'll show you the way.'

The shed was at the bottom of a lawn surrounded with bright plants and flowers. Mrs. Hardy took the key from a hook under the low hanging eves and opened the door. The women were immediately hit with a pungent smell and reeled back. Barbara reached to slam the door shut but before it closed she saw a very strange plant covered with bright orange flowers.

She called her boss and suggested he bring Dr. Arnold Price and his team along.

By nightfall the Pathologist had discovered that the pot plant had been grown by grafting several very rare species of South American plants that Hugh had found amongst Arthur Hardy's preserved specimens. From his notes it was to have been a present for Mrs. Hardy for her birthday. It turned out to be one of the most poisonous plants and had never been seen outside South America - and it didn't have an antidote.

Hugh had returned to his flat pleased with himself at propagating an unusual plant for his friend Mrs. Hardy who had been so good to him. Before long he began to feel unwell, then before he had time to seek medical help, he became paralyzed and died two days later, in excruciating pain, unable to call for help.

Barbara and Mrs. Hardy were taken to the local hospital and put into isolation and checked they didn't inhale any of the deadly poison from the plant. They left two days later with a clean bill of health

Mrs. Hardy felt so upset she had not been around to help Hugh that she sold up and went to live with her sister. Despite Barbara telling her she also might have died, Mrs. Hardy felt guilty about Hugh, and about the fact her proposed birthday present had in fact been a poisonous pot plant and been grafted from something her husband had preserved, for the rest of her days.

Dr. Price and his team were quite pleased to have a new toxin to study and try to work on discovering an antidote.

CUTHBERT AND THE THESPIANS

Cuthbert skulked unobserved backstage, hiding from the comings and goings of staff and pupils in a busy school rehearsing the end of year concert. He was hoping an enthusiastic teacher or child would not discover him and rush up crying, 'Here he is! Cuthbert, we need you.'

The end of term was fast approaching. Teachers were putting the polishing touches into each class's contribution to the Christmas Concert. Pupils were severely warned that unruly behaviour would not be tolerated. Costumes were fitted and altered.

Cuthbert did not like being involved, yet every year since he arrived at the school was somehow press ganged into taking part, no matter how much he protested.

As the year advanced, the prodigious event took over the school and the community particularly in the last term; each year the show was growing bigger and attracting more attention from the local media. It was rumoured that there might be a camera crew from the local television station this year.

Everyone vied for starring roles and the chance of their picture in the paper. The reason given for the annual concert was to raise funds for the school but actually the English teacher was a frustrated thespian who felt she had missed her vocation. She loved the drama of fulfilling her true path in life. Miss Potts did a really great job and produced a show worthy of local amateur theatre. She felt the strain of making each year's show better than the year before. This year she had written a collection featuring many favourite children's stories, carefully picking the songs to go with every scene.

For the last four years there had been a 'surprise' twist and appearance of a mystery guest. People began to try and guess what the character would be and in which scene the 'star' would appear. This year they had a quiz on the programme with a prize for the person in the audience who picked where the mystery guest's character would appear.

Nerves became more frayed as opening night grew closer. Malicious tricks were played as each class vied for the best places in the line-up on the programme.

Cuthbert, quietly avoiding rehearsals and his usual spots around the school, carried out his duties but managed to escape costume try outs and interruption to his quiet life. He felt very smug.

Opening night arrived, parents, families, friends and members of the community streamed into the large school hall. Jostling for prime seats was competitive and some Nannas with age and experience on their side, were very quick despite limping with the aid of walking sticks. At a crucial moment, sticks were abandoned and a quick side step secured a seat near the front.

Tension rose to fever pitch backstage. In true showbiz fashion, 'before the performance nerves' got the better of everyone, lines were forgotten, imaginary sore throats were discovered. Miss Potts rushed everywhere keeping calm thanks to a large vodka and tonic thrown down her throat beforehand, (no smell of alcohol on her breath) – hearing a suspicious noise she crept behind the scenery and pounced on Cuthbert.

'GOTCHA,' she hissed, triumphantly if not grammatically. She dragged him to the costume room, and arrayed him in his finery. Holding firmly to Cuthbert, she cornered James who was playing the lead role in the final scene.

'Right James, you hold on to this creature as if your life depends on it and not only will you get applause at the end of the show, but I'll give you twenty dollars. Cuthbert, behave!

James smiled triumphantly. 'Well done, Miss Potts, don't worry – I'll make sure he makes it on stage.'

Applause rang out, music to Miss Potts and her assistants' ears as class after class performed perfectly, sang in tune, remembered their lines and didn't knock the scenery over.

The curtain opened on the last Act and showed a backdrop of old London town. Striding on stage was James dressed as Dick Whittington, the Mayor of London, and in his arms, a furious Cuthbert arrayed in soft boots, scarf and waistcoat.

Once again the large ginger tom who was employed as the school's chief mouse catcher and comforter of the new entrants, had appeared in the annual concert. He received rapturous applause from his fans. James tickled him under his chin, Cuthbert stopped struggling and found that he quite liked this attention after all – on cue he jumped lightly from James arms, shook off the boots on his front paws, walked to the edge of the stage, sat down and began washing his paws.

Camera lights flashed and Miss Potts felt the adrenalin rush of applause as she graciously accepted a bunch of flowers and acknowledgement of yet another success.

A CUP OF TEA GRAN?

ROGER gazed at the apparently sleeping figure of his Gran slumped in her armchair. 'Either the chair has got bigger or she is shrinking,' he mused. He had surprised the old lady turning up for a cup of tea a day earlier than usual.

His Gran had brought him up when his Dad had upped and left one Friday, taking the contents of her biscuit tin with him. The month's rent, money for the tallyman, and all the other allowances she put by each time she got paid for the little jobs she did. It was the only time Roger saw his Gran cry. He never knew if it was because his Dad had gone or because he had stolen her hard earned money.

Roger was fond of her he supposed, his Gran was the only family he knew. She kept herself to herself and gave her grandson as good an upbringing as any other youngster growing up during the fifties in the city; but really Roger brought himself up. He listened and collected information as if it was currency. He kept his head down at school, did what was asked of him, didn't shine but wasn't bottom of the class. Kept out of trouble. But there was one teacher he remembered.

'I think you are holding out on yourself young Roger,' Mr Gaston had said. 'I believe you are smarter than you're letting on.' But Mr. Gaston had too many pupils to try and educate and when Roger didn't respond to his efforts to encourage him to study harder and show an interest in improving his grades, he soon gave up.

As usual Roger looked around before he left to see he hadn't left anything behind. Then he surprised himself by kissing his Gran's cold forehead. Shutting the door firmly behind him he walked off and didn't look back.

He always walked a different way home. Somehow it made him feel 'in charge.' If anyone was keeping tabs on him, they would never work out where he was going or if he was meeting anyone.

Before he went into the Hen & Chicken Pub where he had arranged to meet his contact, Roger threw the old biscuit tin into a builder's skip after removing the contents and stuffing them in his pocket.

Sitting at the bar he saw Blinky come into the pub. Blinky had had a few too many punches to the head, and after being knocked out once too often, couldn't stop blinking. Without acknowledging Roger he sat down.

'Got the readies?' he asked.

'I've got it all,' said Roger.

'Have a bit of a windfall did you?' wheezed Blinky.

'You could say that,' said Roger. He handed over part of the contents of his Gran's biscuit tin. He had looked in the tin last month when he visited and couldn't believe there was two thousand quid in there. Enough to make the new life he craved for in Canada.

Blinky handed him back a note with Roger's name on it. He had missed seeing it tucked amongst the banknotes. He opened it and read his Gran's spidery hand writing.

Roger, I have been adding to this tin every year after I paid my way since your father left. I thought that one day you might either need it to settle down or you'll do what your Dad did and rob me blind. I hope I will be giving it to you and wishing you the happiness you never had growing up. I didn't have it in me to give you the love a boy needed but I did care, Roger. However you get this money I wish you a better life than I or your Dad gave you,

love Gran.

Roger sat at the bar frozen for a moment then screwed the note up and put it in the ashtray. He turned to Blinky, picked up the envelope left on the bar beside his drink. He quickly checked that the contents were exactly as promised, finished his drink and turned to walk out of the bar. Half way to the door he stopped and careful as ever, turned back, leant over the bar, picked up the crumpled note from the ashtray and put it in his pocket.

Two days later he got off the flight from UK to Montreal and began a new life with a new identity. It seemed by shedding the past he became a completely different personality, outgoing and involved in his neighbourhood and community. He married and was a caring considerate husband and later a loving and kind father to his son and daughter.

From time to time the memory of the small figure in the armchair, how cold her skin felt when he kissed her forehead and the note she left; invaded his dreams but he shook them off. He considered it was a price he paid for freedom from his past...

A BUG - NOT IN A RUG

CAITLIN used to think that 'flying things' with a wingspan wider than the opening of her ear couldn't possibly fly in. But not anymore! She was wrong!

During the middle of one Sunday night she catapulted out of bed with the onset of an excruciating pain in her left ear accompanied by a mad fluttering noise and sensation that something was dancing on her ear drum. After ten minutes of shaking her head wildly, and hitting the right side of her head trying to dislodge whatever was causing the pain, she gave up and decided to drive to A & E at the nearest hospital.

Leaving a note for her flat mate, Caitlin drove off into the night, yelling from time to time as the pain increased. She checked into the emergency department of the hospital and was admitted by a very nice English nurse who did not quite reassure her by saying she might have a burst ear drum, and apologising in advance for the wait because the department was flat out with emergencies, they were short staffed and it might be a couple of hours before she was seen.

However, not long after she arrived a young nurse looked in her ear and was thrilled to see a live bug in Caitlin's ear. She had never seen a live bug in a patient's ear before. Fletching a doctor who looked about fifteen, after he looked in the offending ear, he exclaimed triumphantly, 'It's a moth!' Then proceeded to excavate her ear with, it seemed, a shovel and rake accompanied by screams and bad words in a foreign language by the patient.

Eventually he said 'we'll have to drown it.' He fetched some oil and proceeded to pour it into her ear. Just then alarm bells sounded and he dashed off to another department to help with someone in more pain that she was.

Caitlin called after him as he ran out the door

'How long does it take to drown a moth?'

His reply echoed down the hall. 'I don't know, I'm not a vet.'

Good answer Caitlin thought, but not of any help to me.

It was beginning to take on the making of a comedy skit except she wasn't laughing. In spite of an earful of oil, trying to keep still and hoping the moth couldn't do the breast stroke she was still in pain.

After waiting patiently for half an hour wondering if they had all changed shifts and forgotten the drowning moth and her lying there in distress; the nurse who had admitted her turned up and said someone would be with her soon.

Vikram, the young doctor looking as if he was just out of school, failed again to remove the offending creature and said,' I'll have to get the Senior Consultant to look in your ear.'

The Senior Consultant was apparently too senior to come down to Emergency so Caitlin was ushered down long corridors and into the 'senior presence.' More checking, vacuuming, syringing, accompanied by more wild screaming (a little more subdued this time as Caitlin felt in the presence of a more experienced medical person) yelling bad words in a foreign language, (much more acceptable than in English) wasn't very polite; he finally declared, 'You'll have to go up to ENT department, they have more specialist equipment. They should be able to see you in a week.

Caitlin almost screamed again at the thought of putting up with stabbing pain for a week.

The Senior Presence saw the look of horror on her face and said, 'Well one more try with warm water then.' He poured water into the offending ear, it was cold, probed again, and then held up some tiny forceps with the dangling, limp body of what was once a moth. It had felt at least the size of a bald eagle.

In great relief, first that it wasn't a burst eardrum, second that the wild life had been removed from her ear. Caitlin thanked the Senior Consultant, and suggested to Vikram the young doctor that if he was going to use a spade and a rake perhaps he should take up farming. Everyone laughed, Caitlin a little hysterically.

LETTER TO MY SOULMATE

Dear Michael

I thought of you last week and smiled. I was clearing out my box room, I'm moving house again and spent an afternoon browsing through a lifetime of memories.

In an old suitcase was a record of our time together. Photographs, maps of our trips across the world, scraps of restaurant bills, programmes from rock concerts, and the glass jar full of sand from the middle of the Sahara Desert that we collected just before a sandstorm trapped us in our tent for three days. Looking at it reminded me of the sheer terror I had felt when I realised that nobody in the world knew where we were and if something happened we would have just – disappeared.

We did have a very special time growing up. Looking after each other at school then surviving the turbulent years between leaving home, going to university, finding part time jobs and travelling in the holidays. Finding our dream jobs which turned out not to be exactly what we wanted and moving on. Eventually settling down and becoming 'responsible.'

What happened to us? Where did the years go? I believe what we shared was unique. I think we truly were soul mates; what a pity we didn't fall in love, but there was no passion between us, just the very best of friendship. Remember the night you thought it was your duty to make a move on me? We had just finished a bottle of very rough red from that little café in a fishing village south of San Sebastian in Spain. It was a glorious moonlit night and we had our tent pitched near the beach. Very romantic! I collapsed in giggles when you kissed me and your manly pride was wounded until you began laughing too and we cried with laughter. Our friendship moved up a level from that moment. No wondering if we would get married and settle down, just understanding and looking out for each other.

Remember when I fell for that completely unsuitable Erich from Cologne. I was obsessed and every time he let me down, you were there to mop up the tears, pat me on the back and make me laugh again. When you met Margie from Liverpool, you were certain you couldn't live without her, until she disappeared suddenly with your credit card leaving you with all the bills.

Snapshots in my memory bank of that beautiful scarlet and gold sunset when we sailed out of Tunis towards Palermo in Sicily – flamingos flying across the setting sun with their pink wings and white feathers striking against the cerulean sky. We were speechless with emotion at the beauty and drama of Nature - unable to put feelings into words I felt that my heart was filled with love for the world and my eyes were full of tears. We watched North Africa disappear from view and the sun disappear as the small ship sailed towards Italy. A magical time of our lives.

I never felt so completely comfortable with anyone as I did with you Michael. Not even with David, my husband, and I did love him, nor any of the rest of my family. Maybe we were born under the same star or were twins in a previous life. We talked about anything together and knew the other would never criticize or judge what we said.

Whatever the explanation, thank you for being there for me; sharing without words at times, just a look or a touch of the hand, meant you understood what I was feeling. Holding me tight when I was emotional about something, making me feel reassured and safe. Even though eventually your life took you to the other side of the world to settle down, and raise your family with Sara. I stayed in Scotland, married David and raised my family. Memories of the years we spent together, through school, then our adventures travelling and working in different parts of the world would pop up over the years and give me courage to keep going when times were a bit tough.

When I heard from you last week saying that you and your family were visiting UK, would be in Edinburgh and asking if we could meet up I was really happy. I was so looking forward to catching up with you again and meeting your family. I wanted so much to see you again maybe for the last time in our lives.

Then the phone rang yesterday, James our old college buddy calling me with the news. I couldn't believe what he said.

The love we shared Michael was deeper than any passion, absolute acceptance of each other. Thank you for being part of my life's journey, for teaching me so much, for understanding me, listening to me, helping me see another side of a problem; the laughter we shared, the courage you gave me to face anything life threw at me.

Love and safe journey,

Until we meet again.

Jane

(Next day Jane stood in the foyer of the church then followed directions to the quiet room she was looking for. Gazing down at the still figure in the coffin she bent and kissed his cheek then tucked the letter she had written to her best friend out of sight down the side of his cold body.)

ESCAPE FROM MARRAKESH

Bridget woke to another cold wet morning in her tiny bedsit in Earl's Court, London. She looked out of the window at a grey dawn. Raining again; had it been 'forty days and forty nights of rain?' It seemed to have been pouring forever. Before getting out of bed she looked again at the photograph her friend Julie in New Zealand had sent her. It was taken along Kiwi Esplanade in Mangere Bridge; her toddler son was playing with a friend on a little beach. The tide was in and sparkling in the sunshine. The children were laughing and tanned from the sun. Bridget felt an overwhelming yearning to feel the sun on her skin and bones, warming her through. The memories of walking along the waterfront past the bird reserve to Ambury Park Farm brought a smile to her face.

Jumping out of bed, she turned on the small gas oven to help the spluttering heater bring some warmth into the compact little bedsit, which despite the chill, she loved. Bridget had 'getting ready for work and out the door on time,' down to a fine art. Porridge cooked while she had a very quick shower, clothes picked ready the night before to struggle into, eat her porridge and drink a cup of strong coffee while applying her make-up. She had a small pretty face; her mum's green eyes looked back at her from the mirror together with her father's shock of thick red hair. Half Irish and half Welsh she had a double dose of Celtic genes.

Although born in Wales, Bridget arrived in New Zealand at six months old, when her parents immigrated. Her dad had the offer of a good job and they wanted to give her and her siblings a better life. They lived in Auckland and during holidays and long weekends often went camping or out on a day trip to one of the Islands in the Hauraki Gulf. By the time Bridget was a teenager the family had visited most of New Zealand, with the occasional trip back to see family in Ireland and Wales. But she'd always wanted to go back to the UK and when she earned some pocket money and began part time work in school holidays, she always saved some for her OE travels. Once she had finished her studies she began making plans. Her family had paid her fare as a 21st birthday present.

So here she was, two years in London and loving it. Emailing home shortly after she arrived she said, 'I love every speck of dirt on London's sooty face.' Always a history buff she hugged to herself the knowledge that streets she walked in the city had, over thousands of years, been walked by people who changed history; wrote books she loved, people of courage and those who caused devastation and loss. She walked in the footsteps of Charles Dickens, Shakespeare, Winston Churchill and all the people who fascinated her from history, and dreamed that one day she, in some small way, could be part of changing history.

With her degree in Computer Science and Programming she got a job with a small specialist team working out of an office in Canary Wharf. The office was part of a company contracted to the Security Services. After the shock of 9/11 and watching horrifying television coverage of planes flying into the Twin Towers in New York; and then the 7th July 2007 London underground bombings, every government was very aware of the threat of terrorism and how vital it was to prevent attacks before they occurred. It had been a long selection process, with her past and that of her family being checked, even back to her childhood in New Zealand. Her team was working on advanced security systems for future roading, rail and airports around the UK. The idea being that all major countries eventually would have even better systems in place to help each other with tracking terrorist cells all over the world.

Making sure the stove and everything else was switched off, Bridget checked her mirror before going out, all spit spat and Bristol fashion, as her Granddad, an ex-Royal Navy man, used to say. She felt cheerful; it was Friday and she was meeting her friend Polly this evening at the Rising Star pub near where they both worked. James, her neighbour in a house full of bedsits, was leaving at the same time. A cheerful Australian; they looked out for each other, took phone messages, collected mail and had the odd drink together when they had time. Running down the road catching up with what they each had been doing, they plunged into the bowels of the earth at the Earls Court Underground. James went one way and Bridget the other to catch the route to Canary Wharf. She quite enjoyed travelling by tube, unlike many people she chatted to, but somehow this morning she was more aware of warning notices reminding people to be vigilant and look out for unattended bags or parcels. Shrugging off an uneasy feeling, Bridget got off at her station and hurried out into the rain and round the corner to her office.

She was soon engrossed with the team and the project they were working on and the day flew by.

Just before 5pm Polly phoned to check she was still coming to the pub. 'I've got a fantastic opportunity for us to get out of this rain for four days, away from the cold and into some sunshine. I'll tell you all about it in the pub; can you check with your boss if you could have a couple of days off?' Polly worked for a travel agency and from time to time managed a cheap trip for them when someone had cancelled.

'I'll try,' Bridget said, 'I'm not sure if he will agree but I am flavour of the month, as I came up with a new way of looking at the project we are working on. See you soon.'

An hour later, Polly and Bridget were sitting tucked away out of sight of the usual Friday night crowd in their favourite pub, enjoying a bottle of award winning New Zealand Pinot Noir from Villa Maria.

Bridget and Polly had met over a year ago. Although very different personalities they had hit it off and become firm friends. Polly, with her long blonde hair and bright interested face, exuded confidence. She was a little overweight but it didn't worry her, 'more to cuddle,' she would say with a giggle. Although she looked the typical 'dumb blonde', Polly was far from dumb. Her instinctive intelligence was there behind the good time façade. She could sum up someone she had just met to a tee and rarely was taken in by someone pretending to be what they weren't. She enjoyed being invited out by the young men about town, some who thought they were onto a good thing, but if they took for granted that a night would end in her bed; she hopped in a taxi and went home to her small cosy flat where she enjoyed living alone. Not that she was averse to a night of unbridled passion, she confessed with a giggle to Bridget, but it would be a mutual decision.

Since meeting they had shared nights out at the theatre, dinner or when an unexpected cancellation came up at the travel agency Polly worked for, they flew off for a few days to Spain or Portugal or for one memorable night to an open air concert outside Rome.

Both girls enjoyed their jobs. Bridget loved the challenge of working with a team she respected, knowing they were accomplishing something worthwhile. Polly loved organizing and matching holidays for people who came in looking for 'something different'. A world trip, a cruise or hiking in the Himalayas. She was respected by her employers and in line for promotion to manager in the near future.

When they had settled in their seats, discarded their coats and scarves and taken a satisfyingly large drink of wine, Bridget said, 'OK, tell me all about this chance to get out of the rain for a few days.'

Polly replied, 'Remember I told you about the chap who came into the agency last week; it was quiet and everyone was out to lunch with me holding the fort?'

'Yes, I remember, you told me he was a rather fine specimen of a man, someone worth a second look.' Bridget smiled at her friend.

'Well he told me he was thinking about buying the agency. I was a bit shocked at that as I hadn't heard anything from Simon and Hugh, the owners. As far as I know they are doing well and seem to be happy with the business. Anyway, his name is Aamir, he is from Tunisia or Algeria or somewhere from that neck of the woods. Speaks beautiful English, must have gone to Oxford or Cambridge or at least had an upper crust English nanny. He said he had been interested in the company for a while and had made some discreet enquiries and that if he did decide to buy then he wanted me to stay on as manager.'

Bridget gave her a thumbs up. 'Sounds good, or does it?'

'I'm not daft Bridgee as you know, but he really convinced me, and asked that I didn't mention it to anyone else in the office or talk with the owners for a couple of weeks, as by then he would have made his mind up whether to go ahead or not.'

'Where does our weekend away come into it?' said Bridget. 'It all sounds plausible but you will check it out won't you, Polly, as far as you can?'

'I've decided I'll go along with this weekend and then decide. He said that he and his family want to add some five star hotels to the travel business they own, and want someone to go and check out a prospect they have been considering, in Marrakech! All expenses paid and flying business class! I'd have four days' stay in this five star hotel, as a tourist, to check it out, see how efficiently it's run and make a report. He also asked if I had a bright friend who would help as it would look better with two friends having a few days holiday together. I immediately thought of you and said I have a clever friend who works in a hush-hush job in Canary Wharf and would certainly notice if things weren't run properly.' Polly sat back looking pleased with herself.

Bridget was dismayed. 'Oh! Polly you know I asked you not to mention what I do to anyone.'

'Oh! don't be silly Bridgee, he doesn't care what you do, all he wants to know is if the manager at the hotel is on the take and if the service is five star and good enough for his company to spend mega bucks acquiring.' Polly was persuasive and allayed Bridget's concerns.

Bridget shrugged. 'Well we do say we have to take a chance in life Polly, so if you feel he is genuine let's do it.'

The two friends laughed excitedly at the thought of an unexpected break from work and rain and began to make plans.

Saturday afternoon and the girls were in the British Airways lounge at the airport waiting to board their flight to Morocco, destination

Marrakech. They hadn't eaten much all day and they lunched on the lovely food provided, finishing up with a glass of champagne while celebrity watching. They wondered where the great and the good, the sports stars, TV and movie personalities, were flying off to and to which hideaway in the world, away from the prying eyes of the media. Just before going to the boarding gate, Bridget went to the ladies. On the way back she made a phone call to James. She suddenly wanted someone to know where she was going to be for the next four days and when she was due back in London. James took down the name of the hotel where she would be staying and her return flight number.

'I'm green with envy, Kiwi,' he said cheerfully, 'getting out of this weather for a few days. We'll have a drink and you can tell me all about it when you get back.'

Before long they were being ushered into their large comfortable seats in Business Class, offered another glass of champagne, magazines to read and menus to decide what they wanted to eat for dinner.

'This is the life,' said Polly with a sigh of pure enjoyment, as they settled back to enjoy the flight.

Just over three and half hours later they touched down at the airport in Marrakech. The sun was setting as they flew over the Atlas Mountains and the amazing buildings below took their breath away. They had carry-on baggage only, so cleared customs quickly. In the arrival area they spotted a tall, immaculately dressed man holding a sign with the name of the hotel where they would be staying. He quickly walked up to the girls and introduced himself.

'My name is Mustapha, I will drive you to your hotel, come with me.' He hurried them out to a large waiting limousine.

After they were settled into the back seat of the air conditioned car and Mustapha had driven off quickly, Bridget said quietly, 'How did he recognize us Polly?'

'Don't worry; I'm sure Aamir sent him our description.'

'But he didn't know me. Did you tell him what I looked like?'

Polly hesitated, 'No, but he must have described me and said I would have a friend accompanying me. Don't fuss, Bridgee.'

Soon they were driving up to the most beautiful hotel they had ever seen; past a wonderful landscaped pathway, meticulously tended gardens, fountains, and a huge swimming pool, to arrive outside an elegant entrance. Floodlights from the ground lit up the walls of the building. It was like walking into another world. At reception a beautiful girl smiled and welcomed them, and when their names were entered into the computer, a door opened and out stepped a tall swarthy man. He had a hawk-like nose and his dark eyes seemed to bore through them.

'Welcome Madams, I hope your stay is a pleasant one, please call me if you do not have everything you need.' He gave them a plain card with his name and extension number and then disappeared through the door as quickly as he had appeared.

After a wonderful night's sleep in what turned out to be a suite, with two king sized beds, a bathroom almost the size of Bridget's little bedsit, and a lounge, the girls woke early eager to get on with the day. They enjoyed a beautiful breakfast, taking note of the service and the food; they couldn't fault anything to put in their report for Aamir.

'Right let's behave like tourists and go to the Medina and walk around the Souk. I've heard 'fabulous feedback about what you can buy,' said Polly with a smile.

'Great idea, I'll just go up to our suite and pick up my bag,' Bridget stood up.

'Righto!! I'll have another prowl round and see if anything needs improving and meet you at the entrance.'

Humming to herself, Bridget waved the room card to get into their room. She hesitated inside the door, feeling something wasn't quite right. She thought she heard a noise. Without thinking, she pretended Polly was with her and began talking as if she wasn't on her own.

The room was empty.

I must be paranoid, muttered Bridget to herself, and then she stopped in front of her bedside table. Something was different. Taking out her smart phone, she checked the pictures she had taken of the rooms and had sent to her Mum and Dad back in New Zealand. The guidebook she had been reading the evening before wasn't in the same place. It had been moved slightly, but definitely moved. The room hadn't been serviced as they had hung the "Do Not Disturb" notice on the door handle. Still chatting as if Polly was with her, instinctively she picked up their passports and documents, put them in her zip-up bag and hurriedly went down to join Polly.

Bridget waited until they had cleared the hotel grounds before telling Polly of her concerns. They had turned down an offer from "Hawk Eye," as Polly irreverently called him, to be driven to the Medina.

'We want to walk and see everything on our way; it isn't far, but thank you.' Polly gave him what she called her "blonde smile," widened her eyes, tossed her hair back, and watched as she almost read his mind, "silly little fool."

Polly initially dismissed Bridget's concerns, believing that she may have knocked the book after she took the photo. 'But what about the noise I heard? I am sure someone was either in the bathroom or lounge. I wasn't going to investigate just in case,' said Bridget.

Polly was quiet for a moment, 'Maybe they have got wind of the proposed buyout and what we are really here for and wanted to get some information about us.'

Then for a short time their worries left their minds as the sights and sounds of the Medina hit their senses as they pushed their way through the crowds. When they got nearer the Souk they were assailed by colour, traders shouting, musicians playing, stalls with shoes, bags, clothes, carpets and most of all the wonderful smell of spices, dates, exotic fruit and cooked food. Although Bridget was as fascinated as Polly at everything around, her senses were alert and picked up they were being followed. Suddenly, she grabbed Polly's hand and pushed through the crowds down a quieter alleyway away from the main Souk. She was right; there were definitely footsteps behind them. As they turned round a bend in the alley, a figure with long robes stepped out of small shop selling jewellery.

'Quickly Madams, in here,' he whispered as he put out his arm and pulled a curtain aside. For some reason they trusted him. The girls stepped inside and stood silently in the dim light. Outside they heard an angry voice shouting loudly in Arabic. They heard a soft mumbled reply then footsteps running back the way they had come. Their rescuer stepped behind the curtain and said in perfect English, 'All clear, did you know you were being followed?'

'What's going on?' demanded Bridget, 'how did you know we were being followed?'

'Because we were following your followers,' answered their knight in flowing Arabic robes.

'Now you're frightening us,' said Polly with a shake in her voice. 'We are entitled to know what is going on; surely it isn't because we are checking out the hotel for a proposed takeover is it?'

'Nothing so mundane I'm afraid, much more dramatic than that. Sit down, I'm waiting for someone to join us and he will explain everything.'

A few minutes later from the back of the little shop a figure appeared.

'James!' Bridget could not believe her eyes, 'what are you doing here?'

The man in front of them looked very different from the slightly scruffy Aussie who lived in the next bedsit in Earl's Court. In a light linen suit he had an air of authority and looked serious.

'Surprise,' James smiled at Bridget. 'We hadn't planned on you knowing who I was just yet, but circumstances have suddenly changed with your unexpected trip to Marrakech. Now Polly, you need to sign the Official Secrets Act. Bridget has already signed when she began work for the Security Services.'

Polly thought for a moment and with her intelligent take on the situation decided not to argue about what was going on. She signed the paper.

'We can't tell you too much girls, but enough to say that Aamir is not thinking of buying the travel agency where you work Polly, but he contacted you to get to Bridget. They had planned on kidnapping her and getting the results of the work she and her team have been working on. A terrorist attack is being planned when the G8 leaders arrive in Britain next year.'

Bridget went white.

Polly grabbed her hand. 'I'm so sorry Bridgee, I'd no idea.'

James said, 'There was no way you could have guessed. Aamir is a very clever man and has fooled many people Polly, not only you. We got wind of what was being planned and when you phoned me Bridget, we put things together as we are aware he has contacts here in Morocco, particularly in Marrakech. I have to ask you if you are ok to carry on. We will be close by and have people in the hotel watching you twenty-four hours a day; you will recognize them by this little pin they are wearing.' He showed them a tiny silver fern. 'A nod to your New Zealand connection, Bridget,' smiled James, making them feel a little more relaxed. 'Also both of you take these very small cell phones, there is one emergency number programmed in, and if you are in any way concerned or in danger, just press the connection and someone will be with you as quickly as possible. We will understand if you say no as it is very dangerous, but it would be of tremendous assistance in clearing up this part of the terrorist network.'

The girls were silent as they took in what James had told them.

Then Polly spoke up with a glint in her eye. 'I'm game, Bridget. I never thought I'd be working for Queen and Country! James said we will be taken care of, and this is an opportunity to tell our grandchildren "what we did in the war against terrorism"– seventy years on of course James,' she grinned.

'Great disguise that dumb blonde look Polly, you are a clever girl,' said James.

'I'm in too,' said Bridget. 'I knew these sort of things went on but I never thought I'd be involved, only behind the scenes with my work. I'm pleased to help "in the front line," James. But tell me, why were you in the bedsit next to me pretending to be an Aussie?'

'We'd got wind that the people we were keeping an eye on had plans to get at one of the team you worked with, so we kept an eye on you all. Then it became apparent with Aamir's approach to Polly who they were targeting.'

'OK, we'd better get moving; you have been out of sight too long. Felix here will show you out the back door and where to get to the main part of the Souk. You'd better get shopping to have something to show for your trip to the Medina. When you get back act as you normally would and enjoy the facilities. Just keep chatting, but be alert to who is around. Remember your room is probably bugged so be careful what you say. We do want to pick up this cell of agents working here. A good team will always be close by; our priority of course is to keep you both safe. Remember, in an emergency if you are at all worried just press the button on the cell phone.'

'Got it,' said Polly. 'Sounds exciting.'

'Don't be fooled Polly,' said James, 'it's not a game, these are seriously bad people.'

'Sorry James, I didn't mean to be flippant, I will be sensible and we will look out for each other,' Polly said apologetically.

Bridget told James about feeling uneasy when she went up to their suite after breakfast and had taken their passports and documents.

'Well done,' said James, 'best let me have them just in case we need to get you out quickly.' After slight hesitation, Bridget handed them over.

'One last thing James,' asked Bridget, 'where's that Aussie accent gone?'

James smiled and said in a soft Irish accent, 'Oh! I'm very good at fitting into a part me darlin', accents are one of my specialties.' He kissed them both on the cheek and said seriously, 'We're very grateful, but keep safe and we will be watching out for you.'

Following Felix through the narrow alleys to the main part of the Medina, he slipped away before they reached the myriad of shops where the owners cried out to them, waving their goods and trying to entice them into their tiny shops. The girls forgot for a short time what James had told them and bought bright colourful wraps, long robes, slippers and jewellery. They arrived back in the hotel, unaware of anyone following them, although they knew there would be someone shadowing them with Felix and his team hopefully behind.

As they walked into the elegant cool reception area, they were immediately met by a beautifully groomed young woman. 'Ah! Madams, you have enjoyed your visit to the

Medina, I see by your bags you have been shopping,' she smiled. 'I am Sarah, in charge of looking after our guests, we want to ensure everything is to your liking, can I offer you some mint tea in the little courtyard and you can tell me how I may help you, and if you are enjoying your stay in our hotel?'

Thinking quickly Bridget said, 'Thank you Sarah, we would love to join you, let us drop our parcels up to our lovely suite, freshen up and we will be right down.' Sarah hesitated but had to agree and said she would wait for them in the courtyard, pointing to where they could find it.

Going up in the lift Polly said, 'Whatever happens don't let them try to separate us, we need to stick together.'

'Yes, and make sure we have our cell contact to James, just in case.'

They put their packages on their beds and chatted casually about how fantastic the Medina was, aware there might be a bug in the room, before they freshened up and went downstairs.

'Ah! Madams,' Sarah greeted them as they came into the lovely sheltered courtyard. A table was laid with pots of tea and glasses beside each place along with trays of dates and figs, nuts and tiny pastries. Brilliantly coloured blossoms on the table finished the setting.

'Please sit, enjoy the tea and tell me did the beautiful Medina meet your expectations and how you are finding your stay in the hotel? We are all very proud to be of service to our guests.'

'Thank you,' the girls said together, grateful to sit after their adventurous morning.

After enjoying the refreshments and chatting to Sarah, saying all the expected good things about the hotel and the Medina, they saw ''Hawkeye'' come into the courtyard.

'Madam Bridget, there is a call for you from New Zealand, it sounds urgent.'

Without thinking how her parents could have got the number of the hotel, and that it was the middle of the night in New Zealand, Bridget jumped up and followed the man. Polly went to follow her but two men appeared from the shrubbery, one held her arms and one put a hand over her mouth. She was pulled out of sight, behind the trees. Remembering her self-defence training, instead of struggling, she leaned towards the men and dropped, making herself heavy. It threw them off balance and they stumbled, allowing Polly to shake herself free and run towards the reception area.

'Bridget,' she yelled urgently, just before she was grabbed again and hustled over to the lift.

As Bridget went to go into the office to take the reported phone call, she hesitated. 'I'd like to take the call in my room if you don't mind, please transfer the call.'

She turned and ran up the stairs to the fourth floor where the suite was. When she burst into their rooms and heard a moan from the bathroom, she was horrified to find Polly lying on the tiles with blood pouring from a head wound.

'Be careful, watch out,' Polly whispered, barely conscious.

Bridget reached into the pocket of her kaftan and pressed the button on the cell phone, just as she felt everything go black as a hood went over her head.

The emergency cell rang and James, who was with Felix and their team preparing for all eventualities, picked it up and listened.

'Damn! There is nothing, but I picked up some noise and the sound of someone moaning before it disconnected. Bridget and Polly could be in trouble. The group must have got wind we are around and took action sooner than we thought. We'd better get moving; send a signal to

Ali at the hotel and find out what he knows. Let's move.'

Ali, whose real name was Brendon and whose cover job was janitor, worked out of the basement of the hotel and picked up the signal to find out what was happening. He alerted the others on the team in the hotel to check the girls' room and any evidence of where they could be. From his work room he picked up the sound of the cellar door opening at the other end of the long area under the hotel.

He slipped out of sight behind a cabinet. He heard the door open quietly and a voice say, 'he's not here, he must be doing a job in the hotel.' Another voice Ali recognized as the security manager, known to the girls as Hawkeye, said 'Get them down here, we only have a short time to make the girl talk.'

Brendon silently sent James a code on his cell telling him where in the hotel the girls were being held. 'You'd better hurry,' he added.

Bridget and Polly regained consciousness at the same time, wrists tied behind them, lying on the floor of a dark room. Polly's head had stopped bleeding but she had a splitting headache and her mouth was dry from loss of blood and shock. Bridget managed to shrug and wriggle out of the hood and was horrified at the state of her friend.

'Listen Bridget,' whispered Polly. 'They want to question you about your work, so let's pretend I am you, then I can't tell them anything. I am not sure how long we'll get away with it, but it might hold them until the cavalry arrive.'

'I can't let you do that Polly, God knows what method they'll try and you have suffered enough.'

'Bridget, listen to me,' whispered Polly urgently, 'they could torture you, or inject you with a truth drug. I can pretend I have amnesia from the hit on the head - that could hold them off for an hour or so.'

Before Bridget could argue any more, the door opened and three strangers came in. Two were wearing Arab scarves round their neck and the third, a suit.

'I see you are awake, you little trouble makers. We are going to sort you out, you need to do what you are told at once or you will suffer as you have never suffered before.' The shortest of the three men appeared to be in charge.

Polly said the first thing that came into her head. 'I can't think straight from that bang on the head, I'm not sure who I am, all I know is I need to go to the toilet urgently.'

'You're not in your hotel suite now,' he snarled again. 'Squat in the corner if you have to.'

'But she is injured. I'll have to help her and I'm not sure if she can walk. Please, undo my hands.'

'Forget it; you're just wasting time. Which one of you works for the security services?'

'I do,' both girls said. There was silence for a moment. The men muttered between themselves.

'Very clever, you're trying to waste our time. But if you don't tell the truth we'll find out in five minutes which one we are going to question.'

Again the girls said together, 'It's me you want to question.'

In a fury one of the men hit Bridget across the head, with such force she fell unconscious to the floor.

'Well,' said Polly, 'if it is me you want to question it's too bad as I can't remember anything before this morning, so if you want to know where or what I do at work, you're out of luck.'

'Get a bucket of water,' snarled the man in charge, 'we don't have much time, hurry up.'

The man who had hit Bridget hurried out of the door.

Outside Brendon took him by surprise, knocked him senseless and handcuffed him to a waste pipe, securing his mouth with tape. By then James and Felix had appeared and the three men went silently to the door where the girls were being held. Brendon had the bucket in his hand when he opened the door, and as the man in charge turned to demand why he had taken so long, Brendon hit him hard and jammed the bucket on his head. Sadly for him it was full of waste product from a leaking pipe. Felix quickly took care of the last man standing while James checked Bridget and Polly.

'Bridget, wake up, are you OK?' his voice was grim.

Coming to, Bridget thought for a moment they were back in London in her bedsit. By this time Felix and Brendon had secured the two men. Some more of the team arrived and collected them, whisking them and the man they had previously handcuffed to the waste pipe through the back entrance of the basement to a large black armoured truck which had blacked out windows.

Caged inside were five others, including Hawkeye, handcuffed and trussed like stuffed turkeys.

James said to Felix, 'I think we have the main members of the cell but I can't be totally sure, so we need to get the girls out of Marrakech as soon as we can. We can't risk going to the airport, so we can travel half way by road, be picked up by our backup and taken to Tangier. We'd better wait until dark.'

Smuggled out of the hotel in robes covering them from head to toe, Bridget and Polly were taken to a private villa near the Medina in the old part of Marrakech. After a warm scented bath and a doctor tending their bumps and bruises they felt much better, but were eager to get on their way back to London.

'Just try and relax girls,' said James. 'We are not out of danger just yet. We are going to travel to a destination in the Atlas Mountains where we will be picked up by a new team, and hopefully arrive in Tangier sometime in the morning. Then we will find the quickest and most secure way back to Blighty. You'll be pleased to hear that our men back at the hotel have managed to bring us your things and all the shopping from the Medina!'

A week later James, Felix, Bridget and Polly were sitting in an obscure office in Whitehall; talking with an unremarkable looking man with a quiet voice who took them over everything that had happened during the past month, from when Aamir first approached Polly, to their encounter in the basement where they had managed to keep any information relating to Bridget's job from being extracted from her.

Mr. Jones, as he had been introduced to them, was very complimentary and told them that that particular cell group of terrorists had been swept up and it would take their leaders some time to recover. The rising tide of extremists was becoming more and more difficult to stop, but the powers-that-be were very grateful for all their help. It couldn't be acknowledged publicly of course but an ex-gratia payment of a significant sum would be paid into their accounts which would, in a small way, help their future.

After they were politely dismissed, James and Felix took the girls out to dinner in a quiet, very expensive restaurant hidden away from the social set. They didn't talk about the previous few weeks, but enjoyed each other's company and wonderful food and wine. Polly sparkled and Felix couldn't take his eyes off her. James and

Bridget chatted and found they had a lot more in common than they had discovered when James was the Aussie living next door.

'It is going to be hard going back to routine,' said Polly as they left the restaurant.

'Oh! I don't think it will,' said Bridget. 'It has been something I am very glad to have been part of, although I wouldn't want it to happen too often! An experience to remember; and I think now I may have fulfilled a little dream I had of making a difference.'

James planted a kiss on her head. 'You certainly did, you can both be proud of yourselves. We certainly are, aren't we Felix?'

Felix didn't reply. He was in a clinch with Polly which indicated there might be more excitement ahead!

THE STALKER

'I'm sure I'm being stalked! Those late night phone calls are freaking me out!' Jodie said dramatically to her friend Frankie. They were on the same shift this week and were catching up over lunch in the canteen.

'Who can it be?' asked Frankie. 'Have you been upsetting anyone lately? You can get a bit snaky when you are annoyed.'

'No I haven't,' retorted Jodie indigently, 'but it's getting a bit scary.' Her voice became a little shaky and Frankie showed a bit more sympathy.

'Maybe you should report it to the police,' she said.

'And say what?' asked Jodie, 'about four or five phone calls over the last few weeks at different times of the night, no one speaking, once I heard a faint scrabbling sound?'

'Would you like me to come and stay with you for a few nights and if whoever it is calls again we can take a note of the time and see if we can hear anything?' asked Frankie.

'Oh! Thanks Frankie, you're a pal, I'd appreciate it if you stayed then you'd know it isn't my imagination.' Jodie replied gratefully.

'We'll get to the bottom of the mystery. Here, it's like Miss Marple, or Inspector Frost. We'll make a list of who calls you from time to time, who you know and see if we can come up with a name,' Frankie said enthusiastically.

That night when the girls were tucked up in sleeping bags in Jodie's bed-sitting room, cups of cocoa, crisps and chocolate biscuits at the ready, they began to look through Jodie's address book. They tried to work out if there was a clue about who might be either playing a trick, or desperately trying to get hold of her. Or, as they didn't like to consider, were trying to frighten the living daylights out of her for some unknown reason.

At about midnight the girls dropped off to sleep and slept through until the alarm at 7 am. Frankie was rather disappointed after getting psyched up for the phone to ring in the middle of the night. Jodie was rather relieved.

After their shift finished that day they went to the pictures to take their mind off mysterious phone calls and got back to Jodie's bedsit early evening, settled in and waited for the phone to ring. Three in the morning and the girls woke to the sound of the phone ringing. Both of them had their hearts in their mouth as Frankie grabbed the phone and yelled, 'Hello, hello, who the hell is this – why are you phoning, who is it?' Silence at the other end, not even heavy breathing. Tears began to run down Jodie's face. She had had enough and was terrified.

'That's enough,' said Frankie, 'we are going to contact the phone company and police in the morning, you're a wreck Jodie.' Frankie put the kettle on and made some tea while they planned what they would do before going into work.

Six o'clock, the phone rang again. This time Jodie grabbed the phone, with Frankie there with her she felt angry at whoever it was phoning, disrupting her life and frightening her half to death. 'Who is it, why do you keep phoning me, what do you want?' she demanded, yelling into the phone.

This time a voice said 'Jodie is that you?'

'Who is it,' she stammered, not quite recognising the voice with the delay on the line.

'Hey Jodie, it is Joe from Australia, have you been getting any phone calls lately?'

'Yes, yes I have! What do you think you are doing, calling in the middle of the night scaring me half to death and not saying anything?' by this time Jodie was yelling.

An embarrassed Joe answered, 'Well, it wasn't me, it was my cat.'

'What do you mean, your cat? Don't be daft, I have been terrified and was about to contact the police, afraid to go to sleep. I've had a friend come to stay with me to keep me company. How could your cat dial my number?'

'Well I got this new phone a few months ago, I had nothing to do one night and I programmed in everyone's number in my address book to speed dial. I've been working long hours lately and my cat has been on its own and got lonely. Anyway he had been playing around, knocked the phone off the hook and played with the buttons on the keypad. He must have hit your speed dial number and listened to the dialing of your number. Clever thing, he found someone to talk to him.' Joe sounded admiring of his clever cat. 'I've had a few people complaining about calls from my phone, they had caller ID so they knew it was from mine. I thought I'd better call other people on my speed dial and check.'

'Hang on Joe, I just have to tell Frankie, she has been staying with me to keep me company as I have been so frightened, I thought I was being stalked!'

'Gee I'm so sorry Jodie,' her cousin Joe grovelled, 'I'll sort it and put the phone in a drawer so Samson can't play with it again. I'll make it up to you when I come over to visit. Is it the Frankie we used to go to concerts with before I left for Australia? I'd like to see her again, say hello from me?'

They talked about when Joe was arriving, and he promised next time she heard from him, he would be on the other end of the phone.

Frankie and Jodie sat over cups of coffee and toast, talked about the unlikelihood of a cat phoning, then laughed until tears ran down their faces with relief at the stalking mystery being solved.

When they left home for work Jodie linked arms with Frankie and as they ran down the road to catch the bus she laughed and said, 'That's one for the books, having a cat as a stalker!' With spirits lifted, the girls were looking forward to seeing Joe in a few weeks and began to plan where they would take him.

'I think I'll book tickets to see the musical "CATS" as a surprise, laughed Frankie.

SPEED BUMP

Alice's face slammed into the steering wheel. Searing pain made her eyes water and putting her hand up she felt blood trickling down her face. For the first time in her driving life she had driven off without fastening her seat belt. She pulled into the side of the road and turned off the ignition. Tears of pain and frustration ran down her face as she fumbled for tissues in the glove box. Last time she drove along this road there wasn't a speed bump!

Alice lost consciousness then when she came to, opened her eyes and focused. Everything had changed. She blinked. The modern dashboard of her Ford Fiesta had disappeared. It was replaced with the basic dashboard and steering wheel of a Ford 10. Lifting her eyes she saw the trees were smaller and fewer. There were hardly any houses around. The road was unsealed and very rough.

Someone opened the driver's door and looked in.

'Grace, are you ok? What happened? Why are you driving Fred's car?' A young woman looked anxiously at her. 'It's me, Sheila, don't move - I'll help you out.'

Alice felt herself being carefully helped from the car and sat down on the grass verge at the side of the road. She couldn't focus properly. Why was she wearing different clothes?

The woman who had helped her out said gently, 'Do you think you can walk with my help? We need to get that cut on your head cleaned up.'

There was a little cottage across the road and the woman who introduced herself as Sheila half carried the injured Alice into the kitchen and helped her onto the sofa. She felt herself drifting off into unconsciousness. Next thing she knew she was floating up towards the ceiling, where there was a wooden clothes pulley over the black range cooker with washing airing. She found herself sitting on it and looking down as a man came into the room. Why were they calling her

Grace? What was she doing sitting up here? Was she dead?

Shelia was wiping the figure on the sofa's brow and saying anxiously to the man, 'Fred, you need to get the doctor, I can't bring her round, and I'm worried she might be seriously injured. Why was she driving your car?'.

'We'd had a row,' Fred answered, 'and she just drove off. I'm sorry Sheila, it was something about nothing. I've been worried about not getting work with the baby coming and all. I'll go and see if the car is ok to drive, if not maybe Mrs O'Flanigan up the road can do something, she helps a lot if anyone's sick.'

'Ok Fred, take it easy, I'll look after her. You try and get the car moving and get to a phone or drive into town and see if Doctor Grey will come out. I'll send Jonny up to Mrs O'Flanigan's house to see if she can come down.'

Sitting on the pulley Alice looked around the room and saw a photo that she recognised. It was a bride and groom smiling at each other. She looked closer. It was a photo she had seen many times at her Gran's house while she was growing up. Something familiar that she hadn't really looked hard at for years. It looked just like her. Longer hair, old fashioned shoes, the groom was in army uniform. Shocked, she looked again at the figure lying on the couch. *It was me,* she said to herself, *or is it Grace? Am I dead?*

She remembered scraps of conversation with her Gran about her sister Sheila who had helped her and looked after all the family after their father had died in the First World War, and her mother when the 'flu' epidemic swept through New Zealand in 1918. Alice tried to remember what she had told her and felt cross with herself for not really listening properly although she was interested. She remembered her Gran's name was Grace.

Mrs O'Flanigan arrived and went straight over to where the injured Grace (as Alice thought of her now) was lying. 'Pregnant is she?' she asked Sheila.

'Yes, Fred just told me, how did you know?'

'Experience,' replied the middle aged woman. 'What happened to the lass?'

'We're not sure, I saw Fred's car at the side of the road and Grace slumped over the wheel, she must have had an accident of some sort. Fred said they had had a bit of a blue and she'd run out. He's gone to see if he can get the car started again and fetch Dr. Grey.'

By this time Mrs O'Flanigan had given the unconscious young woman the once over, checking there were no bones broken. She was more concerned about the head wound with the possibility of concussion and any harm to the baby. After cleaning the wound on Grace's head and putting on a bandage, she asked Sheila to fetch blankets and towels in case the baby was lost. Searching in her bags of pills and potions, she took a small bottle out asked Sheila to fetch her some cooled boiled water. She put some drops into the water, then lifting up Grace's head she put the liquid to her lips. She managed to get a little down her throat, then kept trying until most of the liquid was gone.

'We've done all we can,' Mrs O'Flanigan said. 'We just have to keep her still and warm and hope the doctor isn't too far away.'

Alice found herself flying through the air to where Fred was desperately trying to get the car to start, his head was under the bonnet and Alice looked over his shoulder. She saw a plug had popped off just out of Fred's line of vision. She popped it on firmly, then went round to the driver's seat and pulled the starter button. The car shuddered and began to tick over. Fred looked up in astonishment and wondered for a few moments how it had started by itself. Then he slammed the bonnet down, leapt into the car and drove off.

An hour or so later Fred and Dr. Grey arrived at the cottage and hurried inside. Alice sat smugly on the mantelpiece watching as the Doctor examined Grace. Just then Grace stirred and sat up asking the classic question, '*What happened, where am I?*'

'You're a very lucky young woman,' said Dr. Grey. 'If your husband had been a few hours later you might not be here, and of course thanks to Mrs O'Flanigan and Sheila for doing all the right things. I think you will be ok now and don't need to go to hospital, with the excellent care you have here I'll think you'll be fine in a few weeks.'

Fred saw him out and Alice heard the doctor talking to Fred about how he got the car to start after it had been in an accident, then told him his car was out of action and when he had taken him home could he have a look at it? At the back of Fred's mind lurked the thought he didn't know how the heck he got the car to start, but he'd give it a go.

'Sure Doc,' he said, I'll be happy to check it over.' From then Fred's career as a motor mechanic took off and as he made a little money he bought books and went round garages to get an idea how the mechanics of cars worked. He thanked his lucky stars that however his car started on that eventful day it changed their lives for the better.

Once Grace was no longer unconscious, Alice began to feel faint. She managed to float outside, across the road and watched as the side of the road rose up to meet her.

She vaguely heard a car door open and Mike, calling urgently, 'Alice, Alice, speak to me Alice, I've called an ambulance.'

She felt herself being lifted out of the car and put down on the grass verge.

Later that day she came to in a hospital bed with her Gran sitting by her bed.

'Oh! You're awake are you love? Mike has just gone down to get some coffee, he has been beside himself with worry. He told me your news, about the baby, I'm so happy for you both.'

Alice smiled and gripped her Gran's hand. When she felt better she was going over to her house and ask her all about her life with Sheila and Mrs O'Flanigan and look at all her photos. She suddenly knew that her baby was a girl and her name was Grace.

ERNEST AND HENRY

(This is the first chapter from a proposed novel set over 100 years, beginning with Ernest and Henry. I am planning to complete it by next year)

'Well I must say Henry, that is a grand job you have done finishing that park bench,' said Ernest. 'You've done just what I told you and more. It is a real pleasure to see the workmanship.' Ernest smiled at his young apprentice. Henry coloured bright red at the unaccustomed praise.

'Thanks, Mr. McIllvenney, I enjoyed making it with you, I remembered what you said about the pleasure it will give folks for years to come when they sit under the trees in the park on this bench.'

The bench was the last job Henry would be completing under the guidance of Ernest. He had been called up to join the Army, it was 1914 and war had been declared on Germany. Ernest was too old to sign up and he was planning on joining the wardens to assist and use his knowledge as a master carpenter to do all he could to help.

'Well,' said Ernest, 'we may as well be the first people to try the bench out. Let's get our lunch and mug of tea. We probably won't have much time to chat as you are joining your regiment next week.'

Ernest sat down stiffly and Henry handed him his mug of strong black tea from the billycan. Then he joined him on the park bench and unwrapped his lunch. Leftovers from last night's dinner; a small piece of meat and a dumpling, a hunk of bread with a tiny piece of cheese. There was a small piece of cake to finish.

'Your Mum is good to you young Henry,' said Ernest smiling at him.

'She is that,' replied Henry, 'and it is a hard job feeding six of us with Dad out of work. After his injury when that big accident happened at the factory, there is no one will take him on. He feels so helpless, but at least I earn a bit and will get half my pay from the Army sent home.'

The old man and his apprentice sat on the bench they had just finished and thought of the past few years working together. Ernest was a kind and patient teacher and Henry, although a little slow sometimes, picked things up and carried out what was asked of him. He showed an extra flair in finishing a project. Also he had an instinct when seeing a lump of wood turn into a useful or beautiful piece of furniture and had a feeling of pride that he had helped fashion it.

'I shall miss you Henry,' said Ernest. 'You've been a pleasure to work with and now you're off to fight for your Country. I hope you come safely home. I fought in the Boer War in Africa and saw sights men shouldn't see. I don't know what's ahead for you and all the other young men of England and our Empire, but know I will be thinking of you and of the day when we can sit together again on this bench we made and you can tell me how you've managed.'

'I'll write to you Ernest, oh! Sorry I mean Mr. McIllvenney.'

'No, Ernest is fine; you are a craftsman now, and going to fight for King and Country. I am happy for you to address me as one soldier to another. I'd like to hear from you and how you are going on.'

A tall thin young man appeared in front of them hung about with boxes and bags.

'Do you gents mind if I take your photograph?' he said. 'The paper is writing about young men joining up and I hear from the Council that you are joining your Regiment next week. My name is Jim Dickon and I work for the Daily Press.'

The men agreed and Jim suggested Ernest remain sitting on the bench and Henry standing behind, leaning on the back. He put them at ease and had them smiling at something he said. 'Now hold steady, it could take a minute or two until the flash goes off.' Jim disappeared under the blanket-like material draped over the camera. A little time later the flash went off and Jim appeared from behind the paraphernalia and beamed. 'That's a good 'un – I bet it will be in the paper tomorrow. Now tell me about yourselves and which Regiment you are joining Henry?'

A little while later, Jim had the background on Ernest and Henry. They had got quite talkative and Jim reckoned with satisfaction he had a good story there to add to the others he had gathered.

Henry and Ernest tidied up after Jim had gone and then Ernest said 'Do you know Henry, I think the bench would be better over there under that little grove of trees. It is sheltered from sun or rain and anyone wanting to sit and think will be protected.

They picked the bench up and carried it across the grass until it was settled finally in the exact spot Ernest thought would be best.

'Let's try it out,' he said, 'and you tell me Henry what you think you will see when you get to France and what you might like to do when the War is over.'

Henry began hesitantly, how he was afraid of what was ahead, he had never seen anyone dead and hoped he would be brave and not let his Regiment and family down. He leant forward, elbows on his knees, and somehow for the first time in his life he found the words to express what he was feeling and his concerns for what lay ahead; if he would be brave enough, strong enough. How in the middle of the night since he had signed up, he woke in a sweat thinking if he could just run away and hide and forget about the war, everything would be alright.

As he talked on, words pouring like a burst dam, Ernest sat quietly beside him, a familiar steadying figure in his life, until he felt stronger and the fears slipped away. He turned to Ernest with a smile and said.

'Thanks Ernest, I feel much better. I don't think I have ever talked so much in my life. I am not sure what you said but I know I can go off to fight and I won't disgrace you, my family or my Regiment.

He put his hand out to pat Ernest on the shoulder and froze. The old man was leaning back on the bench, his head to one side and he had a little smile on his face as if he recognised someone who was waiting for him.

A week later, Henry in his uniform sat on the park bench before he joined the Regiment for training and thought about Ernest's funeral. He looked at a copy of the photograph Jim had taken of them shortly before Ernest had died. They were smiling and it was a good likeness of them both. He looked closely at the photograph and saw around Ernest's head a faint aura of light.

Ernest had only an elderly sister left. His wife and son had died many years ago. Ernest's sister had given Henry his prized tools, telling him, 'my brother often talked about you and I know he would want you to have his tools and that you will use them well.'

Henry was touched and carefully stored them away at his parents' home ready for him to use when he returned from the War.

He felt Ernest's presence on the bench they had made together and thought about how he had somehow given him the strength to grow up and move from being a young apprentice full of fear and apprehension to a soldier fighting for King and Country. 'And for men like you Ernest,' murmured Henry, 'you've given me confidence to face my fears and not let myself down. I'll remember all you have given and taught me.'

Henry folded the photograph carefully and put it inside his jacket, shouldered his kit, nodded to the bench and marched off to the railway station, to camp and take on a soldier's duty.

SEE YOU IN PARIS

'See you in Paris.' The sign in the travel agent's window advertising a package deal of a trip for two to Paris triggered memories which took the middle-aged woman back to her early passionate determination to save the world, or at the very least to be part of making a difference.

'See you in Paris,' a throwaway comment Sally made after the march through London in the 1967/1968 protests. Exhilarated at the end of the day of protest, before going home Sally had called to the others the four words which, they repeated every time they met. Somehow it reminded them of what they were trying to achieve.

The next big protests planned were the so called barricades' protest in Paris. This was a time in history where a revolution swept through the world. The old left leaning towards being slightly pink if not red, parents now of children declared the older generation had sold out to the establishment. Everything was being questioned. The immorality of war, civil rights, apartheid. John Lennon sang Revolution and the atmosphere was of energy, demands for change. As well as being encouraged to tune in, get high and drop out.

'See you in Paris' became a catch phrase they used when they met at university, at meetings for the next protest march. The four friends had met at London University, all of their parents had encouraged them to have the education they had not been able to have. It was an exciting time to be alive and Sally, Eric, Bryan and Rose became involved with student protests, determined to do their bit in changing the world.

They'd been born after the depression, the horrors of War, and didn't know the struggles of privation, with little money, no jobs and very little hope. Full of youthful energy, stirred by injustices they felt needed changing. With increasing prosperity and the availability of material things which made life easier, they didn't really understand what the previous generation had survived.

Sally sat in a café opposite the travel agent's, ordered a coffee, and thought about travelling to Paris with her friends and dozens of other students and young people to join French students staging a huge protest about all the things they were fighting against. On the ferry from England they were exhilarated, felt they were going to take on the world, no one could stop them and of course they would win, achieve all the demands they were making. Who would refuse them?

They didn't have much money between them and once they arrived in France, bought some bread, cheese and a couple of bottles of cheap red wine and began to hitch hike. A large truck stopped when they had Rose (who had long legs, short shorts, and wild red hair blowing in the breeze) stand in front with her thumb out. On the truck were more students the truckie had picked up, they climbed aboard and joined the others. Someone had a guitar, they began singing, spirits were lifted, food and wine shared. By the time the truck reached Paris the young people were intoxicated not only by the rough wine but with their combined energy and determination.

A day later they were holed up behind barricades, throwing anything they could at the police, yelling demands and insults. Sally and her friends were shocked when the Parisian students began hurling Molotov cocktails at the police. The police hit back, students were beaten and Eric who, filled with the drama of smoke, noise, and yelling, suddenly leapt over the barricades and ran towards the police line screaming at them to stop. They retaliated, thinking he was carrying a weapon. He fell and didn't move.

Sally, Rose and Bryan collected Eric's body from the authorities several days later and one of the major newspapers in UK paid for their return journey to London in exchange for their story.

Somehow their passion drained with the shock of Eric's death, the violence on the streets instead of just the rhetoric they were used to hearing and repeating. Rose didn't finish her degree, she went back to Edinburgh and married the boy she had been going out with before deciding to go to University in London. Sally and Bryan did carry on with their studies, but didn't see each other very much after Eric's funeral.

They met several years later. Sally was working in advertising and quite enjoyed her job. Bryan had found it difficult to focus but eventually became a hard headed financial consultant for a major banking institution. They married and were briefly happy for a short time, eventually divorcing a couple of years later. Ghosts invaded their dreams.

Sally came out of her reverie and realised an hour had passed. Leaving the café she once again glanced across the street at the words 'See you in Paris' and resolved to phone Rose and Bryan and try and lay those ghosts from the time of turmoil when they were young and passionate, and see if they could return to their friendship before the revolution.

THE CAT CAME BACK

James sat on the old seat he had made fifty years ago when he and Annie had moved into the house they bought when they married. Tomorrow he would have to say goodbye to the home and memories of a lifetime shared with Annie.

The house had been a bit of a wreck when they moved in, but both had a vision of the home they would build together. The view was something they both loved; the sea, rolling hills, bush and mountains in the distance. James had carved a seat from an old tree trunk lying at the bottom of the property and when they had finished a day's work scraping and cleaning the walls they sat outside eating dinner, drinking in the sunset and sounds of the sea in the distance. They talked about their plans for the future and the family they would have. Always they had so much to talk about and each seemed to know what the other was thinking.

Five years ago Annie had died and he felt part of him had died with her. He managed well keeping their garden flourishing, enjoying visits from his family and friends from time to time. Then he had a mild stroke. The rural delivery man Joe, who always called in when he went past, found him and drove him straight to the local doctor's clinic. He was transferred to the nearest hospital and before he knew it, was surrounded by his three children and social workers.

He found it hard to believe that his children and the powers that be had decided he couldn't manage alone any longer. There was a lump in his chest like a piece of dry bread swallowed whole.

Thoughts of his granddaughter Katie, who, when she was a little girl looked so like Annie, pushed through the cotton wool of his memory. It was three years or more since he saw her last.

#

Katie was sitting in her borrowed bedsit in London when her mum had called to say Granddad had had a stroke and couldn't look after himself any more. She burst into tears when she'd hung up the phone. This was a catalyst to cause her fragile emotions to spill over.

Eric had left for New York yesterday. Several years ago they had travelled from New Zealand, off on their big adventure, and had a wonderful time exploring all the out of the way places in Britain and Europe not just the big tourist centres. Finding jobs, and in the end she had worked and supported them both while Eric studied and completed his qualifications to get the career he wanted in a big Financial Institution. They had moved into a beautiful flat, as Eric said he wanted to make it up to Katie for supporting him all the time he was studying. Four months later he announced he no longer loved her; he had grown while she had stood still. He had been offered a job in New York and was leaving next week. Oh! By the way Jemima his PA was coming too.

#

Just because my speech was affected a bit didn't mean I was 'do-lally', James muttered to himself. I understand what you are all doing, why don't you ask me what I want? I don't want to

252

leave my home where Annie and I lived together - I just need a little help.

A week later James was sitting at the kitchen table, waiting for his daughter to arrive and drive him to the Rest Home. They had taken Smudge the cat a few days ago, and given him to a family who'd moved into the district and were happy to take an old cat. Annie had rescued Smudge when he was a few weeks old from a hedge and fed him with a dropper until he was big enough to lap from a saucer. James missed the big cuddly cat with the loudest purr he had ever heard. The cat and the man comforted each other when Annie had died.

#

Katie felt numb when Eric went off happily to work the day after he had dropped his bombshell. She packed her clothes and a few treasures which were hers. Changed all the bills from joint names to his name alone, put the keys on the hall table and left. A friend at work was leaving on holiday and her bedsit was available for Katie to stay for a few weeks until she sorted herself out.

The night she heard about her Granddad the tears both for her lost relationship, her granddad having to leave his home, and homesickness combined and she sobbed as if she would never stop. After falling asleep exhausted she slept deeply and in the early morning woke with the strongest feeling her Grandma had been sitting on the seat in the garden smiling at her. She knew then what she needed to do.

Walking up the path towards the home where she had spent many happy childhood holidays, Katie knew she had made the right decision to come home. She would deal with Eric and what she would do with her life later; now it was one day at a time.

#

The gate squeaked open and a voice called 'Hello, Granddad, I'm back,' James looked up and for a moment thought it was Annie walking up the path. It was his granddaughter Katie who he'd thought was in England.

James smiled and suddenly felt everything was going to be ok.

Katie told him she had broken up with her boy-friend and suddenly wanted to be home. She was taking some time out and wondered if she could stay and they could look after each other.

Before he could try and speak there was another noise at the door - a very cross scrabbling and meowing. Katie opened the door and Smudge marched in straight to where his dish should be and sat expectantly waiting to be fed.

James and Katie began to laugh and he said the first proper sentence since his stroke.

'Welcome back Katie and Smudge, everything is going to be all right.'

A FEW DAYS IN COURT

'Ignorance is no Defence in Law,' declared the Prosecutor to the Jury. 'The Legal Ramifications of taking responsibility for money given in good faith and misappropriating it, is an indisputable fact. Despite Mr. Carterton's protestations, he, in plain terms, stole millions of dollars from people who trusted his promise to invest their money, give them interest and secure their savings. In essence he lied. He became more enamoured of the life he and his family enjoyed and used other people's hard earned money to support that lifestyle.'

Margo found her attention wandering. She gazed fixedly at the Senior Barrister prosecuting for the Crown and thought he would have made a very good actor if he hadn't gone into Law. For a moment she caught his eye and blushed, thinking he could read her mind. As Madam Foreman of the Jury she had to pay close attention to what was being said.

A week ago she had turned up as a good citizen for Jury Duty, waited for the ballot and for the third time being called, her name came out of the barrel. The other times Margo had served on murder trials. This case was less dramatic and harrowing but for all that, the machinations of the accused were the stuff of a bestselling crime novel. When the rest of the jurors found out she had served on other trials she was elected Madam Foreman. On a different level it was interesting seeing how the system worked and Margo felt on the whole that trial by Jury was fair. There must be times when it failed, and a lot depended on the eloquence of Counsel on both sides.

At the end of the day, with strict instructions from the Judge not to discuss the case with anyone at home in fact no one, the jurors were advised to be back in court by 9 am next day.

Margo had left her car at home and come in by public transport, she didn't know how long she would be and didn't want to incur outrageous parking charges. It was getting dark when she got off the bus at her stop. A man she didn't recognize from her neighbourhood got off at the same time. Feeling slightly alarmed she took her cell phone out of her pocket and held it tightly. Quickening her pace she heard the footsteps behind increasing their pace too. Feeling quite scared she pressed the single number of her home speed dial number, oh no – it was engaged, one of the kids talking to their friends. What was she going to do?

Two days later after both sides had strongly put their arguments, they listened to witnesses, the Judge had summed up and directed the Jury to look at the facts of the case and put any feelings of sympathy for one side or the other out of their minds. A decision must be made purely on the strength of the case as presented by both Counsels.

After lunch, the twelve diverse members of the public discussed the case. Len who was quite enjoying a few days away from being a car salesman mused aloud, 'Is it illegal if you are caught being dishonest, or if you are not found out, if only small sums of money disappear and no one notices or protests, who worries about Legal Ramifications then?'

Eleven faces turned towards Margo's chair expectantly, 'as if,' Margo thought, 'I have obtained a Law Degree by virtue of having previously served on a couple of trials.'

'Are you talking about someone else Len? This case is about millions of dollars. We can't use idle speculation,' said Margo, 'we have to concentrate on the facts as presented. Did he knowingly steal the money, or was he careless, did he not check advertising and promotion where he gave his name and word to the promises that were made. Did he work alone or rely on other people in the Company without checking on them.'

Michael, an Economics Tutor at University, said, 'as far as I am concerned he is guilty, having transferred all his assets, houses, bank accounts into his wife's name a few months ago, it certainly gives an indication that he knew the axe was about to fall and had better protect the lifestyle he and his family had become used to.'

For the rest of the day they went over their notes, argued back and forth with different points of view.

Margo decided to take a vote and see how the majority felt then work on any doubts the dissenting group had.

'Who believes the Defendant is Guilty, raise your hands.' To her surprise ten hands were raised. So it seemed although there were lots of arguments, most people felt he was guilty.

Several hours later the Jury filed into Court. Margo stood when requested by the Clerk and gave the unanimous decision they had reached. Guilty. The Defendant looked stunned and glared at her.

After being thanked by the Judge and dismissed, the 12 people who had spent the last few days discussing and arguing points of law together, stood in the hall somewhat reluctant to leave each other. It had been rather like being stranded on a desert island and now they were free to go home. Back to the routine of their days and not think of the Legal Ramifications of someone else's actions.

Margo felt sick as she walked out of the courtroom. She found the Clerk of Court and said it was urgent she speak with both the Prosecuting Council and the Judge relating to the case. Shortly after she was ushered into the Judge's Chambers. The man who had stopped her just before she reached home on the first day of the trial, had in no uncertain terms outlined exactly what was going to happen to her family if she didn't find Mr. Carterton not guilty.

In the Judge's Chambers after explaining what had happened, she produced her cell phone, pressed play on the recording and the threats to her and her family were heard clearly. The Judge called for the Detective Inspector who investigated the case and he recognized the voice as someone he'd interviewed on the case. They told Margo she should have reported the threat, but she told them her family had been going away to Sydney early next morning with her husband, so she thought she could safely let the case carry on and the trial proceed. She said it would have been a waste of tax payer's money to cancel everything.

The Judge, Council and the Detective Inspector smiled to themselves, and the Judge said, 'Off the record you are correct, but the safety of your family and jurors come first. We are very grateful for the way you have dealt with this very worrying matter.' The Detective Inspector interrupted to say the offender who had issued the threats had just been picked up.

'Good,' said the Judge, 'it will be a pleasure to send him down for a very long time. After a fair trial of course.' Everyone laughed, Margo with relief.

THE PRAYER

Hang on a mo Charlie,' whispered Paddy.

Two petty crooks were hiding in a timber yard waiting for the night watchman to finish his rounds. Paddy ducked down behind a stack of timber, clasped his hands and closed his eyes.

'Wot's up,' hissed Charlie. 'Wot you doin'?' he said, staring at Paddy in amazement. 'We got ter get into this firm while it's quiet.'

Paddy had his eyes shut, lips moving. Charlie could hear a mutter but couldn't make out what he was saying.

'Nuffink,' muttered Paddy, 'let's go.'

'No, I want to know wot youse was sayin',' Charlie demanded.

'Well, don't laugh,' said Paddy reluctantly, 'but I always say a prayer this time a' night.'

'Wot kinda prayer?' said Charlie, amazed at the vision of his weedy friend, praying!

'Me Mam used to make me say it each night when I wuz young, I just never stopped,' said Paddy, looking slightly embarrassed.

'Every night, even in the nick?' asked Charlie, as a mental picture of Paddy kneeling by his bunk in jail saying his prayers made him snigger.

'Yeah, every night, never miss. I've never broken the habit.'

'Hey look out,' breathed Charlie, 'Car's coming – Hell's bells! It's the rozzers. Let's scarper.'

Later over a bottle of beer in Charlie's room, the Cockney said thoughtfully, 'You know Paddy, if you hadn't stopped to say that prayer, we'd have been nicked. Wot is it?'

Slightly embarrassed, Paddy recited the prayer in a singsong voice.

'Angel of God My Guardian Dear
To Whom God's love commits me here
Ever this night be at my side
To light and to guard to rule and to guide
Amen.'

'Well he guided you tonight all right,' Charlie said admiringly. 'You'd better teach it to me, yer never know when I might have to call on my Guardian Angel.'

'Every bleedin' day, Charlie,' laughed Paddy finishing the beer. 'Every bleedin' day.'

THE WATCHER BEING

WATCHED

A man stood motionless in the shadows watching a woman who was hanging out her family washing. He wasn't aware but a short way up the hill another figure had the watcher in his sight.

The dark haired man who watched the woman and house decided the time was right to make a move. He had plans. Plans that he had put together over many years while he brooded about the perceived injustice handed out by the woman's father to him when he was a teenager. He had been caught running from a burglary gone horribly wrong.

Years ago he had broken into a house he had watched for several weeks. That night he'd calculated all the occupants of the house would be out as usual. He had watched the house and found that every Thursday the four people who lived in the house got into a BMW and drove off to go to dinner, theatre or whatever, he didn't care, they were out of the house.

The young criminal waited for half an hour. One thing he did have was patience. Then crept through the garden to the window latch he had loosened earlier. Climbing through the pantry window, he paused again and listened. Silence. He shouldered his bag, made sure his gloves were on, switched on a torch and began to walk through the bottom part of the house. Climbing the stairs he moved quietly towards one of the bedrooms. Work from the top of the house to the rooms downstairs.

Opening the door and walking into a bedroom he froze – there was a faint sound of gentle snoring from the bed. He was so shocked he turned in a rush to get out of the room and fell over a chair, it made what seemed to be the loudest noise he had ever heard.

A scream came from the direction of the bed. A light came on and the elderly woman screamed louder as she saw the menacing figure before her. The young burglar was shocked at the unexpected disruption of his careful plans. Angry at not having noticed there were only three people getting into the car tonight. He let out a yell of rage and rushed towards the bed, and lifting his torch above his head he brought it down on the grey head of the elderly woman. He had to stop the screaming. He kept hitting until the noise stopped.

Her blood splattered everywhere, over the bed, his clothes, even his face. He turned and ran.

Then there was another noise. The sound of an alarm. Outside the flashing lights of police cars spooked him even more. He rushed to the pantry window and climbed out, shaking with fear and horror.

He didn't get very far, over the fence straight into the arms of two young police officers.

When his trial was over and before the Judge pronounced sentence, he looked into the eyes of the young man in front of him and was silent for a few minutes then said, 'The horrendous crime you committed in battering a defenseless elderly woman to death and your decision that burglary was to be your chosen career path; plus the fact that you have shown no remorse whatsoever, gives me no option but to sentence you to seventeen years in prison.'

Before the Judge could finish what he was saying, the accused spat, 'You'll regret this, you'll be sorry one day.' He was dragged towards the stairs as the Judge said, 'Take him down.'

Every day of the seventeen years he served he went to sleep planning what he was going to do when released. In the library, he researched the Judge's family, what they did and he knew when the Judge retired. He decided his vengeance was to be carried out on the Judge's daughter.

The woman finished pegging the clothes on the line, picked up her basket and went inside. The watcher picked up his bag, checked again; the knife and tape were there.

When he reached the garden, he looked and couldn't see or hear anyone else on the property. He quietly turned the handle of the back door and slipped inside. The sound of the radio was from another room. Walking silently down the hall, concentrating on the room where the noise was coming from, he didn't hear the faint sound of the back door opening again.

Pushing open the door, knife in hand he walked silently towards the woman ironing and singing along to the radio. As he put his hand on her shoulder she turned quickly and pushed the iron an inch from his face, he could feel the heat.

The door burst open and a man rushed in and tackled the intruder. 'Well done Sergeant,' he said to the young woman.

Filled with anger the criminal yelled, 'you're not his daughter, where is she?'

Clicking handcuffs on, the Detective Inspector said, 'Well the Judge was right after all – it was worth keeping an eye on you, in prison and when you got out. He has rarely been wrong in his estimation of young crims like you and your potential to reoffend. It's back to prison for you my boyo.'

Another success for the Prevention of Reoffending Division and for the Judge who was instrumental in establishing the little known Department.

WHAT IF?

'What if, Grandma,' began Will, 'what if when we are born we know or someone picks up what we will be good at in life? What if your family guessed or realized that you would be such a good artist?' He loved watching his Grandma sketching when they went for walks.

Vicky smiled at another interesting question her grandson had come up with. 'That would be wonderful Will, it certainly would save time. On the other hand I think your experience of life helps to make you the person you become and it influences how you look at things.'

She enjoyed when Will came to visit. They didn't see each other very often but there was a lovely connection between them. He was interested in hearing about her childhood in Scotland. How every summer she went to stay with cousins in Ireland. How different life was from his childhood. His imagination was great, he loved reading and looking up interesting facts and fiction and loved hearing about what she and her many cousins got up to during the summer. Vicky had encouraged him to begin writing a diary, just a few notes at first about his day. It became a real interest and she was pleased to see him write a page every night. Maybe he would become a writer.

After Will had been picked up by his Mum and Dad on Sunday evening, her daughter Maggie and husband Bill had an anniversary weekend away. Vicky felt restless and before the sun went down she took Milo, her elderly dog, for a walk. Sitting on a bench along the waterfront she looked out over the peaceful beautiful scene in front of her. The tide was in, birds flying to their roosting places for the night and the sun beginning to dip below the horizon. Her life was ok. She suddenly thought of Will's question. *What if?*

Vicky knew that regret was a useless emotion, there was nothing you could do about missed opportunities, paths not taken. Unbidden, the thought came into her head. '*What if I hadn't emigrated to New Zealand?*'

In the early 1960's, Vicky, after reading a notice in the paper looking for young people who qualified and wanted opportunities for a new life in New Zealand or Australia; followed it up and was accepted. Before she knew it she was packing, saying goodbye to her family and friends and boarding the P & O Liner *Orion* at Tilbury Docks, London. The ship was packed with young single people and families from all over the UK and Europe excited at the thought of a six week holiday on a ship and a little apprehensive at the unknown waiting for them in Australia and New Zealand. Vicky met a group of young people who became firm friends and they still had connections fifty years on.

But, what if she hadn't emigrated, what if like some of her friends and cousins she had stayed in Edinburgh? All her cousins who had stayed behind in Scotland over the years had done well. Gone to university, obtained degrees, married, and owned their own houses, some of them also had holiday homes in Spain or France. A number of times over the years she'd had a couple of trips back to Scotland and Ireland, visiting family and friends. They laughed constantly as they reminisced over old times and the connection was as strong as ever. One cousin commented, *we are like a separate clan - no one else gets us.* Everyone said how lucky she was to live in a country with so much sunshine, less pollution, beautiful scenery. How much they envied her. But she felt there was something missing from her life. *What if?*

Vicky had met and married her husband in Melbourne, a few months after meeting him. Completely on the rebound from a love affair she had had with Sergé, a handsome older man she'd met while working in Paris who'd been the first big love of her life. Sometimes when he'd looked at her she'd lost her breath and they fell into each other's arms, and bed. Only surfacing to go to the bathroom, eat something ravenously, open another bottle of wine, then laughing, tumble back into bed.

Two years of passionate dramas, arguments, making up, him declaring he would never mistreat her again. Then Vicky left him; she wanted to settle down make plans for the future. She loved him and wanted a family, but Sergé was restless; he had been a child born before the War and grew up in the back streets in Paris. Learning with his older sister to survive after their parents were killed, settling down wasn't in his DNA. He was used to being free to do what he wanted and have Vicky around when he wanted her. Months would go by when she was blissfully happy, then he would wake one morning with a black mood, yell and fight and go out and not come home for days.

One morning she decided she would go back to either New Zealand or Australia where she had had a few years of fun with friends when she had first immigrated before going back to Europe. Booking a berth on a cargo ship which had only twelve passengers, she left the following week from Rotterdam. Sergé was shocked out of his complacency and couldn't understand why she was leaving him. *What if, she hadn't left?*

Arriving back in Australia she was shocked at the change of pace from the life in Europe. She desperately missed Sergé and her job in Paris. Missed walking along the streets of Paris. Travelling up to Amsterdam for the weekend, wandering through art galleries and eating in little cafés with lovely food. Laughing and talking with friends, artists and writers.

Then she met Mark. He was lonely, so was she. They came together like two lost souls. They married too soon and Vicky realized very quickly he was certainly damaged, a victim of parents who were also damaged.

A week after they had married a letter arrived from Sergé begging her to come back to him, he loved her and knew that she was what he needed to complete his life. Mark was at work, and Vicky went for a walk and sat on a little beach looking out over the beautiful Sydney Harbour. Should she cut her losses, buy an air ticket back to Paris? She knew she didn't love her new husband, that she had married him on the rebound from Sergé. Then her sense of duty came to the fore and she decided she would try and make her marriage work, Mark needed her and perhaps she could help him.

A year or so after marrying, they had travelled to the UK, worked in London, and their relationship didn't improve. Life was a challenge and a year later they decided to return to Australia. Mark didn't like travelling by sea, so Vicky packed their trunks, and sailed for Melbourne. Mark would arrive a few days before the ship docked.

On board ship Vicky realized how browbeaten she had become. Away from Mark, she talked with other passengers, laughed and made friends. People were interested in what she had to say and didn't dismiss her opinion. Not long after arriving in Australia, she decided she was going to leave Mark – it was unfair on him and her. He begged her to stay and she agreed to try again. Three months later she knew he wasn't going to compromise on anything or try to work together to make their marriage work. He carried on doing what he wanted, so Vicky packed up and left to stay with a friend before flying back to New Zealand where she still had friends.

Not long after arriving in Wellington she found out she was pregnant. Her life as a single mother began. Maggie was the delight of her life and although life was hard financially she loved watching her little daughter grow, and develop her own little personality. Vicky had told Mark about Maggie, he kept promising to come over to visit and get to know her and to send maintenance. Neither promise was met.

Vicky met Joe when Maggie was five and started school. Joe had a small son, in the same class as Maggie, his wife had died of cancer when Micky was two. They all slowly got to know each other, and eventually moved in together. Life was good. They each had learned from their previous relationships, respected each other's interests and were happy when the other wanted to have a weekend or few days away, Joe fishing with friends or Vicky at a seminar which interested her. They never married but their two children called each other brother and sister and were very close.

When the children were twelve, Joe and Micky went away for a fishing weekend. Maggie and Vicky waved them off. Joe had checked the boat and all the safety equipment, they had plenty of food and were well prepared. That night an unexpected wave of bad weather that hadn't been anticipated, hit the coast. Vicky walked up and down while she gazed out the windows at one of the most horrendous storms she had ever seen. She drifted off into a disturbed half sleep in the armchair and woke to the sound of banging on the door. Search and Rescue had received a faint Mayday call a few hours ago. Despite doing what they could they were unable to send up a helicopter or a boat out to search for the vessel in trouble.

The next day she and Maggie waited for news. The search and rescue teams found the wreckage of the boat, Joe's body and miraculously the unconscious body of Micky washed up on a beach miles down the coast. He was near death but the people who found him wrapped him warmly took them to their nearby home and alerted the police.

It was a difficult time for them all, particularly Micky. Maggie was instrumental in getting him back to health. They became closer than ever. She was fiercely protective of her brother and when he got back to school, if he was hassled she dealt with the tormentor. Fortunately Joe and Vicky had made wills a few years earlier, with insurance policies which took care of not only Micky's education but that of Maggie's if either of them died. The rest for the other to ensure they could manage to bring up the children until they were self-sufficient. *What if Joe hadn't died?*

Vicky suddenly realized that the sun had gone down and it was getting cold. Poor Milo was beginning to shiver. She quickly got up and they went home. Milo was happy after gobbling his dinner and snuggling down on his rug beside Vicky. She had poured herself a glass of wine, put out some crackers and cheese, picked up a photograph album from the bookshelf and settled down in front of the fire.

Feeling nostalgic after going over memories of 60 years and more, Vicky wondered how different her life would have been if she had taken different paths, a cab instead of the train, the chance to work in New York. How true that youth is wasted on the young! She thought with a smile, if I could help young people in their twenties to understand that very rarely do opportunities knock twice, often when you think that you will go back and take that chance, it won't be there anymore. Are our lives mapped out when we are born? Are we destined to follow what has been laid out? Or can we find a new map half way through? *What if?*

She looked through the photographs of Joe, Maggie, Micky and herself, of their seven blesséd years together and thanked God or the Universe for every day. Vicky thought that very probably she was luckier than many people who had a life time together but still didn't have what they had crammed into seven years.

A picture she had painted for Maggie when she was about three was tucked into the back of the album. Taking it out looked closely at it. It was very good. Over the years she had often painted birthday cards for friends, written little stories for children for their birthdays and illustrated them. She had loved doing it. Felt a warm feeling of achievement when the picture turned out exactly as she had imagined. Everyone had loved them but she hadn't done anything for years. Vicky remembered Joe saying seriously to her, '*you know Maggie you have a real talent, why don't you pursue it, going to classes or something?*' She never did, partly out of feeling she really wasn't good enough, or where would she start, or she couldn't afford it.

The local community newsletter caught her eye. It was sitting on the coffee table where she had put it to read later. As she picked it up, a box in the top right hand corner caught her eye.

WE ARE LOOKING FOR ILLUSTRATORS TO BRING OUR STORIES FOR CHILDREN TO LIFE. CONTACT US BY COMING ALONG TO THE LIBRARY ON THURSDAY AT 7PM AND SEE IF YOUR TALENT MATCHES OURS!

Vicky felt a frisson of warmth run through her. She looked at the notice again then went to her cupboard where she had a box of some of the cards and children's stories she had illustrated years ago. Looking through them she decided then and there. She would do it. What was that phrase she had read somewhere? If you don't ask you are 100% certain of failure, if you do ask you are 50% sure of success.

As she snuggled into her warm bed with Milo on his blanket at her feet she thought back over all the *What If's?* in her life she had gone over that day and knew that the path she took was exactly right for her. By taking another path she wouldn't have Maggie and Will in her life. Joe and Micky had been such a special part of her journey. The other people and opportunities had help to make her the person she was now and had helped her grow. Now was the right time for her to begin a new chapter pursuing her painting and illustrating and she suddenly knew she was going to be a success.

EDIE AND JOSIE

A Chapter from the novel
THE PARK BENCH

Edwina walked slowly down the winding path of the little park tucked away in a small suburb which she remembered from 50 years ago. She had once taken her children to play here when they were little. She had woken feeling restless. Her 81st birthday was tomorrow and she had been thinking of her past and what the future held.

Mrs. Thingy, (called because Edwina could never remember her Polish name) had come for her daily clean and vacuum. She was very fond of Edwina and fussed around, made her breakfast with coffee and toast just how she liked it.

'What's the matter, Mrs. Edwina?' she asked. 'You are looking a bit fed up today. You want to go shopping? Jan can drive you.' Jan was Mr. and Mrs. Thingy's son who was studying Engineering at University. Mr. Thingy did the garden for Edwina. They had worked for her for years, adored her, and appreciated how well Edwina treated and looked after them.

Edwina didn't like to drive any more as the traffic terrified and bewildered her. So sometimes Jan drove the car and sat and read his University papers while waiting for her to return.

She decided that she would have Jan take her out for a drive. When she got into the car asked him to 'Just drive please Jan, I'm not sure where I want to go.'

'No problem, Mrs. Jamison, just tell me when you want to stop, if you want to shop or take a little walk,' said Jan. He appreciated how Edwina treated his parents, not as employees but friends. The whole family was very loyal and looked on her as a special relative.

Driving past a park she asked Jan to stop and said she would take a little walk and enjoy the sunshine.

Edwina felt tired after a while and was pleased there was a park bench in the shade of some trees with some lovely bushes and flowers in the surrounds. A shapeless figure was slumped at the opposite end of the bench and she felt hesitant, saying to herself, "I hope that person isn't drunk," and sat down as far away as possible. She noticed that a large bag had slipped to the ground at the figure's feet and bent to pick it up. A bony hand grasped her wrist.

'Wot do yer think yer doing pinching my bag?' the figure said angrily.

'No, I wasn't stealing it, just picking it up for you,' stuttered Edwina.

'Erm, sorry, I can't be too careful. Where I live the little horrors are either yelling through my letter box, or stealing my shopping as I come home. I come out here for a bit of peace and quiet,' said the figure.

There was a pause while the two old people gathered their thoughts.

Edwina said 'It is a lovely day, and a nice park, I wanted to get out myself today.'

'My name is Josie, sorry I was a bit rude. I don't get to just chat to many people these days,' said the bedraggled old person.

'How do you do,' said the ever polite Edwina, 'My name is Edwina and I don't get out much myself.' After a pause the other woman spoke thoughtfully.

'Edwina, I used to know a girl called Edwina, but I called her Edie,' said Josie, looking carefully at the other occupant of the bench. 'I met Edie when we wuz in the Land Girls together, during the War.'

'I was in the Land Girls," cried Edwina, 'I worked with a girl called Josie. Is it you? Is it really you Josie?'

The two old ladies stared at each other, their memories going back over sixty years to when two young girls aged about 18, one from a wealthy family, the other from Stepney, learned to dig, drive tractors, and work from dawn to dusk at hard physical work.

'Here, you ain't going to 'ave an 'eart attack are you?' asked Josie as Edwina clutched her chest.

'No, I just can't believe it Josie. Where did the years go? Why didn't we keep in touch? We had such fun together,' gasped Edwina.

'It was bleedin' hard work too, but yes we did have some fun Edie. I often thought of those years together, I think they were the most real part of my life,' mused Josie. 'Here, what about that cute Yank of yours? Did you marry him?'

'Frank, no he went home to his wife in New Jersey!' said Edwina sarcastically.

'Go on, he seemed so lovely, so honest and he was really sweet on you,' said Josie. 'Bastard.'

'Bastard,' agreed Edwina

The old friends looked at each other and creakily began to laugh.

'What about you Josie, are you married, do you have children, what have you been doing for the last almost sixty years?' asked Edwina.

Josie sighed. 'Well I got married not long after the War ended. We had a couple of kids but Harry was always looking for a fast way to make some money. He kept coming up with crazy schemes to make our fortune. They never worked out and I was always working two jobs. Harry's dead I think, he scarpered about 20 years ago and no one has heard from him since. My boy, Frankie, not really a bad lad, a bit like his Dad, and easily led, he ended up in the nick following a couple of wide boys robbing a bank. Janice my daughter is up North somewhere with another bad lot. She is just like her mum, couldn't pick a decent fella.' Josie was quiet for a few moments then continued. 'I'm in a council flat in a block, and it gets worse every year. Sometimes I am too scared to go out.'

Edwina was quiet, thinking about how different her life had been.

She told Josie about how she had married Gerald when he had been discharged from the Army then had joined a bank where his grandfather had been Chairman. He had risen quickly and ended up working in the Stock Exchange in the City. They had lived in Richmond along the river; their children, a son and a daughter, had gone to private schools.

Gerald had been a good husband, reliable, boring. Edwina looked surprised when she said that to Josie; she had never voiced that about her life before. They always did what Gerald wanted, holidays where he wanted, she stopped voicing her opinion because it was soon overridden. Gerry had died one Saturday afternoon at his Golf Club 20 years ago. Edwina soon established a life for herself. A little traveling, she learned Bridge and enjoyed her weekly outing to the local Bridge Club. She worked on the local Residents Committee and found she was good at organizing and fund raising. She often went to the West End to see a show or exhibition. Edwina didn't mind going alone if one of her friends was not available to come with her. After living her life in

287

Gerald's shadow she quite enjoyed pleasing herself and doing what she wanted.

Her son Nicholas was in Hong Kong, something important in the finance world. She could never remember exactly what he did. Married to an American heiress who moved in select social circles. They travelled a lot, had one daughter who was in boarding school in the USA. Nick phoned from time to time to say hello. Edwina wasn't sure if he really wanted to know how she was or if it was duty. She wondered where the little boy who chatted away, loved her to read him stories and used to help her in the garden, had gone.

Her daughter Elaine lived in New York with Steven her husband who was a successful film director and their twin sons. Elaine was a fashion director for a big store on Madison Avenue and was always in meetings, going to meetings or fashion shows. Edwina never knew if Elaine had time for Steven and her sons. Apparently that was life today. Edwina phoned from time to time and talked with Steven and her grandsons, Elaine always seemed to be out. On Edwina's birthday and Mother's Day an enormous bouquet of flowers would arrive from her daughter with extravagant messages of how much she missed her mother and would be over for a visit soon. The promised visit never eventuated.

Edie and Josie sat for a moment taking in the surprise of meeting again after sixty-odd years. Communication was difficult after the war and they had lost touch. Soon they began to reminisce about their life on the farm. The stingy old farmer they worked for. Their strict curfew which they took no notice of when there was a dance on nearby at the American Base Camp. Climbing down the wisteria on the farmhouse wall was no problem. Rationing, remaking their clothes, scrounging soap and cosmetics and listening to the little radio was the main aim after long hours digging, driving tractors and putting up with the crotchety old farmer.

Before they knew it an hour had passed and Edwina said, 'I could do with a cup of tea, what about you Josie?'

Just then a man appeared in front of them, it was Jan.

'Are you OK Mrs. Jamison? You were a long time and I was concerned,' said Jan.

'I'm fine thank you Jan. This is my friend Josie, I haven't seen her for over sixty years,' said Edwina. 'We met by chance sitting on the park bench.'

'Good Morning Mrs. Josie, good heavens, sixty years that's a long time,' said Jan.

Josie looked quizzically at Jan. 'Morning, who's this Edie, your toy boy?'

'No, don't be naughty Josie,' scolded Edwina. 'This is Jan who drives me when I need to go out. Jan, can you drive us to those nice tea rooms near here? We have talked so much we need a cup of tea.'

'Of course Mrs. Jamieson. Can I help?' he said to Josie who was having trouble straightening her knees.

He slowly escorted the vastly different old ladies along the path towards the car park. He settled them into the back seat of the car, making sure the belts were done up, and off they went.

'Oh, Edie I could get used to this, it is a bit different from that old tractor,' and off they went again on a raft of memories.

Jan soon had them settled in Grace's Tea Rooms, then retired to the back of the café assuring the old ladies he had some papers to finish and would leave them to chat. They ordered tea, sandwiches, scones and cakes.

Josie's eyes twinkled. 'Who's paying for this Edie? I'm not sure I have enough.'

'Don't worry Josie, this is an early birthday treat. I'm 81 tomorrow, and this is the best present I could have had meeting up with you again.'

'It is a bit of a miracle all right. I never dreamt when I left my little flat this morning to come along to my park bench I would catch up with my past and remember when I was really alive,' said Josie mistily. 'You know I nearly didn't come out today, I was a bit down. I'm pleased I made the effort, I still can't believe we've met up again.'

They drank their tea in silence for a bit.

'Here Edie, I recognize that glint in your eye, what are you up to now? We always got up to mischief when you got fed up with old grumpy guts Farmer whatsit, and you dreamed up a plan to teach him a lesson or go out on the razzle,' said Josie.

Edwina smiled. 'I have an idea Josie, and I want you to think carefully, tell me if you think it can work. We are both on our own. Our children have their lives and at least I have given up waiting for them to pop in and visit for a day or so and fly off again. You are on your own; you don't feel safe or happy. I am alone, quite comfortable, and Mr. and Mrs. Thingy look after me very well. How long have we got left of our lives? As you said of our time together when we were land girls, it was truly a time in my life I've never felt again. Laughing over silly things, doing something worthwhile, a little bit dangerous, especially when those planes flew over. We never knew if we would be alive next month. We lived through tough and dangerous times but oh! we felt alive, had fun, and we share those memories.' Edwina paused. 'How would you feel Josie if you came and shared my house? We could keep each other company. We could do things together or have time on our own. The house is so big I rattle around in it, so what do you think?' Edwina leaned eagerly over the table and patted Josie's hand.

Josie sat stunned. 'Oh! Edie, I don't know. What if I give up my flat and something happens and your children turn me out, where would I go?'

'Come on Josie, you were never afraid of taking a risk before. I tell you what, we'll keep your flat on for three months, and if you want to go back it is there for you, and I will make provision that if anything happens to me, my family will look after you. Always assuming I go first. I might outlive you,' she said with a smile.

'Take a chance, I think it will give both of us a new lease of life.'

Josie sat for a moment, thought of her fear-filled life at the Council flats with few people to talk to, and then thought of remembering the time of her life shared with Edwina when they were so close they understood exactly how the other was feeling.

'Yes – let's give it a go,' Josie said with the biggest smile she had raised for many years.

'Right,' said Edwina, 'let's go home and see if you like the house and garden, and we will talk some more. You can meet Mr. and Mrs. Thingy then Jan can drive us to your flat to pick up whatever you want. He will make sure the flat is secure and no little toe-rag can break in. We'll have some fun, won't we Josie? Keep each other company and enjoy the rest of our lives?'

There was silence for a moment as the two friends contemplated the idea. A life shared, someone to chat with, a new lease of life.

'Maybe we can even go on a cruise next year,' continued Edwina with a sparkle of something to look forward to.

'Yeah, we might meet a couple of cute Yanks,' agreed Josie. 'Then again, maybe not – bastards!'

'Bastards!' hooted Edwina.

An echo of two lively 19 year olds laughing hilariously sounded as the two old ladies walked a little straighter to the car to begin the rest of their lives.

POOR DEVIL

*(Idea taken from something I read in a very old
magazine from the 1930's)*

Striding up the Champs-Elysées on that wild
October afternoon in 1937, people turned to
watch the strikingly attractive man. He hummed a
frivolous tune from the latest show at the Folies
Bergère.

Under the bright awning of an almost empty
café he spotted a well-built young man roasting
himself by one of those glowing braziers that
French proprietors thoughtfully provided for their
customers on the pavement. The girl beside him
had kicked off her shoes and was demurely
warming her toes. She looked up and her
expression changed.

'Satan, darling!' she exclaimed.

He swept off his hat, bowed and blew her a kiss. 'D'you mind if I join you?'

Eve gave one of her adorable little laughs that always twisted his heart and reached for an extra chair.

Adam got up beaming and shook hands with their old friend. 'We were just talking about you.'

'Talk of the devil, and – hey presto, here I am!' Satan laughed. 'I've just left the Madeleine.'

'There now,' exclaimed Eve, 'what did I tell you Adam? Oh! How I wish I'd been there! The prospective King and the shady lady from the US of A. The smartest and wickedest wedding of the season – everyone is talking about it. I wonder how long it will last. Congratulations Nick!'

'Thank you my dear!' Satan preened.

'Sit down,' she urged sympathetically, 'you look most frightfully cold.'

Satan complied. 'Almost like home,' he murmured, appreciatively spreading himself to the blaze.

'We haven't seen you for ages!' said Adam loudly.

To which Satan bowed ironically. 'About three centuries.'

'Have you been busy?' questioned Eve.

'Very, I'm weighed down with affairs, and all the vices keep getting bigger.'

'If it's not a rude question,' asked Eve, 'what sort of affairs?'

'Routine stuff, mostly. Trying to stop cheap reproductions of my original sin. It's synthetic, like peroxide hair and bad gin. Why can't they be content to sin like decent human beings? I won't stand for it!' he frowned.

He calmed down and looked them both over with a friendly, critical eye.

'Anyhow, it is nice to see you two are still together.'

'We can't help it,' said Eve, 'it has become such a habit.'

'Rubbish,' said Satan, 'haven't you had any temptations?'

Eve gave a little shrug and held out a handful of roast chestnuts. 'Remember what the little brown hen said to the wicked old rooster…' Adam frowned at her reprovingly, and then squeezed her hand. They smiled at each other.

As Satan watched them, something began gnawing and biting at his insides. A twisting pain, which reminded him how eternally lonely he was. After all, they were his particular protégés; his first and only friends when it came to a showdown. They had no right to be behaving so well. Apart from being unethical, it was ridiculous.

He noticed something on the table that looked suspiciously like knitting. Knitting! Not only was it deedsy and homey, but stuffy. As for the pink liquid in their glasses – could it possibly be merely Grenadine mix?

'Damn it,' he muttered and stamped an elegant well-turned hoof. 'They are getting smug.'

'What did you say?' asked Adam.

'Oh nothing,' replied Satan. Then he broke into a laugh, for it came to him in a flash that the thing that gnawed his vitals was none other than Envy.

Satan, however, knew well how to deal with Envy. He welcomed it much as the one-time Boulevardier used to greet his first aperitif of the day. It whetted his appetite.

'Yes,' he mused aloud, after due reflection. 'I'll admit you are still a credit to me.'

'Thanks Nick old man,' said Adam, 'have a drink?'

'With pleasure,' he answered, 'a grog. My withers are shaking like that time we got kicked out into the Glacial Age.'

Eve's heart went out to him, the poor darling, how he hated the cold. Mercifully the waiter came hurrying back with his order. Satan sniffed the fragrant steam rising from the tumbler and put in two lumps of sugar.

'Drink up,' said Adam, 'you'll soon feel better.'

'It might burn me,' said Satan facetiously.

Adam and Eve both groaned. Presently, Adam got up and went inside to play cards with the barman for Satan's drink.

'He's a great fellow,' said Satan smiling indulgently after him.

'How absurd.' Eve's eyes opened wide.

'Not at all, he's lovable and I like his bluff manner,' replied Satan. 'Of course, he can be stubborn as an ox at times, but on the whole we'll call me a sentimental old devil if you like, but–'

Eve raised a small hand to her mouth and yawned. 'Don't Satan, it doesn't suit you.'

'My dear, I'm perfectly sincere–'

'How alarming! Anyhow can you imagine there's a single thing about him I haven't found out by now?'

'Heavens, girl!' Satan exploded, spreading his beautiful hands in mock consternation. 'Don't tell me you're getting bored?'

'Oh dear me, no!' Eve replied and gave him a tolerant smile. 'Only a little, what shall I say, blasé. One can at times have rather a glut of Adam, poor darling. Let's talk of something else.'

'Anything you like. What shall it be?'

'Tell me something about me,' Eve purred.

Satan leaned close to her ear. 'You're adorable. I don't think I've ever seen you look so charming. That dress fits so beautifully, it is just the colour of your glorious eyes.'

'Nick, please,' Eve purred and lowered her long eyelashes.

'You asked for it.' A glint came into his eyes and his voice was like satin. 'Your hair style, it perfectly frames your little face. The last time I saw you, you were almost entirely hidden under a high coif.'

'No dear, that was the time before. We bumped into each other during the Crusades, don't you remember? We discussed the possibilities of picking the lock of Adam's *War Measure*.' She broke off with a reminiscent sigh. 'But you must admit the coif suited me.'

'Of course it did. You have always had the most perfect taste. Even your very first frock made out of almost nothing was intensely alluring.'

'Satan!' she protested, 'will you buy me a drink?'

Satan cast a quizzical eye at her and the contents of their glasses. 'Grenadine, pink lemonade?'

She made a face, putting her head on one side and looking up at him in that fascinating, childlike way that he had always liked so much.

'No, something stronger. That drink was Adam's idea,' she confessed, rather naively.

'I imagined so.' He gave her an understanding smile.

Inside Adam was still enthralled, gambling at the bar, when Satan walked up behind him. He looked worried.

'Losing?' Satan enquired.

'Like hell,' muttered Adam, challenging the barman double or quits.

The fat man behind the mahogany bar threw four kings, but Adam promptly capped it with aces all in a row. 'Ciel! But Monsieur has suddenly the devil's own luck!'

Adam said nothing but gave Satan a wink.

After a moment, Satan began talking about Eve. Among other things, he remarked she was simply enchanting. Like all good husbands, Adam looked suitably embarrassed. 'It's nice of you to say so, but…'

'She's wonderful,' persisted Satan.

A dull expression crept into Adam's eyes. 'Satan.'

'Yes Adam.'

'Let's change the subject.'

'Oh, of course, but…'

'Nick, old man have a heart, I hear nothing but Eve this and Eve that all day long. Understand?'

'Perhaps I do,' Satan replied. 'Then have a drink. What are you having? Grenadine?'

'Lord no! That was just Eve's idea.'

Satan smiled his deep understanding smile. 'I imagined so.'

Soon after promising his friends it wouldn't be another few hundred years before he caught up again, he strolled off, pleased he had stirred some dissension in their too comfortable existence. 'Can't have them feeling they are living in Heaven on Earth.'

MARY'S CHRISTMAS MIRACLE

A Chapter from the novel
THE PARK BENCH

The door slammed viciously shut with the screech of her mother's voice following her. 'And don't come back, we don't ever want to see you again, you little tart!'

Mary buttoned her old coat, picked up her battered case and walked off into the night.

If it wasn't so horrible, it would be a cliché or a script from an old movie, 'the shamed daughter thrown out because she is pregnant and walks down the road while snow drifts onto her head.' Mary thought grimly, wondering where she could go.

There was no one around, it was freezing, and everyone sensible was inside keeping warm, being pleasant to family members before going off to bed. The snow began to fall harder and it was difficult to see ahead.

Turning into a small park nearby and walking along the winding path, she saw a little grove of trees with a park bench. Amazingly it was free of snow and was sheltered from the wind. She sat down and put her feet on her case, lifting them off the ground.

Usually she was a positive girl and could see a bright side of whatever happened. This time however, she couldn't see anything good. She was pregnant, her boyfriend had gone travelling, she had no money, and nowhere to live. Her mother's reaction was one she had expected but it was Christmas Eve and tears began to slide down her frozen face.

Mary thought about Jimmy, the boy she had met at a dance last New Year. It had been such fun. He worked in the office of a local construction company and Mary worked at a nearby shopping centre in a branch of a major book store. They had gone out with a group of friends to the pub after watching a local soccer match, or to the pictures regularly. They had all gone away for a weekend for Kevin's 21st birthday, to a hotel which specialized in celebrations.

They all had a wonderful time, laughing and dancing to a great band, enjoying the fabulous food, drinking too much. Somehow Jimmy had ended up in her bed after the big party, and they had fallen asleep cuddled together still tipsy. During the night he reached out for Mary and they made slow dreamy wonderful love, it was the first time for Mary and Jimmy was gentle and loving. For the first time in her life Mary felt cherished.

Two months later Mary's fears were realized when a test confirmed she was pregnant. Going to meet Jimmy that night she rehearsed how she would break the news to him. He was waiting for her in their usual seat at the local pub. Walking across the floor Mary could see Jimmy was excited, smiling and drumming his fingers on the table. As soon as he saw her jumped up and swung her round.

"You'll never guess Mary; my dreams of travelling are coming true. My company has offered me an opportunity to work with their South Pacific Branch for three years in Australia. I leave next week. This is something I have wanted ever since I first watched 'Skippy the

Bush Kangaroo' on TV. He laughed with happiness. Then said seriously, "I'll never forget you Mary, you are the most wonderful girl I have ever met but this job was conditional on me being single, as it entails moving around and long hours, it is an opportunity I can't miss."

Mary knew she couldn't tell him that their baby was on the way. She opened her mouth but something stopped her from stepping on Jimmy's dreams. A week later, she waved him off, wishing him well with hopes all would go well. Just before Jimmy went through to the departure lounge, he stopped, came back and looked hard at her. "If you want me to stay I will. I love you Mary." He waited for her to speak.

For a moment Mary was tempted to tell him she was pregnant but understood somehow that he would always regret not taking the opportunity. "Oh! Go on with you," she said, trying not to cry. "Send me a postcard. If Oz isn't what you expect I'll be here."

Jimmy smiled, gave her a huge hug, kissed her hard, then turned to run through to the departure area.

Mary took time off work to stay with her Gran up North who had been ill. A few months later, back in London, she bumped into Kevin.

He gave her a hug and said, "We've missed you, how have you been? Dreadful news about Jimmy wasn't it?" Kevin saw the shock in Mary's face and caught her arm as she stumbled. He quickly took her into the nearest coffee bar and ordered coffees; he brought her a glass of water. When a little colour came back into her face he said, "I'm so sorry Mary, I thought you knew."

"I've been away staying with my Gran, I've just got back. What happened, tell me please?"

"Jimmy was killed in an accident in Queensland. The company he was working for were doing some exploratory work and the weather turned nasty, the plane he and three others were in crashed with no survivors."

Mary instinctively put her hand on her stomach as if to protect her baby from the news. Kevin looked at her, realizing with shock her condition, and asked, "Did Jimmy know?"

She shook her head. "I couldn't spoil his chance to follow his dream. Don't tell anyone, please Kevin. I'll manage."

She sat there stunned after Kevin had left, giving her his phone number and urging her to get in touch if she wanted anything or he could help. He didn't leave until she promised.

Sitting on the park bench Mary whispered, "Jimmy if you are up there, look out for us."

A voice said, "Can I help?"

Looking up Mary saw a tall young man with long fair hair pulled back into a ponytail. He carried a small backpack and was reasonably warmly dressed. He took off his jacket and wrapped it round her shoulders.

"No, no I can't take your coat, you'll freeze," stuttered Mary.

The man smiled. "I think you need it more than me. My name is Gabe. Do you need somewhere to stay for the night?"

Mary hesitated, all the warnings she had heard running through her mind, but somehow she trusted him and besides if she stayed outside any longer she would freeze. Anything would be better than this, wouldn't it?

"Yes please Gabe, I don't know where to go and shelter from the weather while I gather my thoughts. Somewhere to stay overnight would certainly be better than sitting out here and maybe freezing to death!" Mary said nervously.

"Right, let's go," said Gabe. "Sister Elizabeth has a shelter behind the old St James Church on Bastion Road. I'm sure she will have a spare corner for you." He smiled and picked up her case. "Take my arm, the paths are slippery, and in your condition I don't know if I would be able to heave you up again." Mary didn't take offence as it was said with humour and kindness.

"Who is this Sister Elizabeth? I'm afraid I'm not very religious and can't remember when I was last in a church," said Mary.

"Don't worry, no card-carrying religious people; the only requirement is you need some help and a bed for the night. Lizzie is amazing and has worked wonders with few resources. She has run the shelter for the last ten years or so. People come and go, get their heads straight, move on to better things. Many have come back to give Lizzie and the shelter some help when they can. A few have stayed as Lizzie is the only family they have. Wait and see, you will be surprised."

With Gabe's firm arm supporting her Mary began to feel warmer somehow and ten minutes later they were knocking on a sturdy door behind the old church. The door was flung open and a thin woman with graying hair scraped back into a bun smiled broadly and hugged Gabe. "Am I happy to see you again Gabe, and on Christmas Eve, how long has it been? Are you back from your travels? Who is this you have brought me?"

Elizabeth's questions tumbled out as she hurried them inside then bolted and barred the door. "I have to remember to lock up; we had a break in last month by a group of young lads high on cheap booze and drugs. Thank God that was the night the Community Constables were making their bi-monthly visit. The boys got more than they bargained for; a night in the cells." Elizabeth smiled.

She steered Mary and Gabe towards the fireplace where a huge old-fashioned pot of soup simmered. One of the group of people around the fire came forward and served up two big bowls of soup and a hunk of bread to the newcomers. Mary's eyes filled with tears and she gratefully tucked into the hot soup.

"There is a bed over in the corner for you Mary, and you can tell me all about how you came to be wandering in the snow in your condition in the morning. There is always a solution, so have a good sleep and don't worry." Elizabeth gave her a comforting hug, showed her where the bathroom was, and put a hot water bottle in her bed.

Mary turned round to thank Gabe but he was deep in conversation with a young man and she didn't want to interrupt. "Please thank Gabe for me. Will he be here in the morning?" she asked Elizabeth.

"Oh yes he will be here. Gabe is amazing, he always appears somewhere he is needed and I'm very pleased he found you Mary. Sleep well, it's Christmas tomorrow and things generally look better after a good night's sleep." With a smile Elizabeth left Mary to get settled down.

Mary woke in the middle of the night with a stabbing ache in her back. She cried out in fright and pain.

Within minutes Elizabeth was beside her. Taking one look at the young woman she said "You are in labour – when is the baby due?"

"Not until mid-February I think," Mary stammered and gasped again as another stabbing pain shook her body.

Gabe appeared and held her hand. "Keep breathing, Mary, and try and relax, we'll help you." He asked Lizzie if they should try and get the young mother to hospital, but she said, "Too late, we'll have to manage here." She smiled reassuringly at Mary. "I think we are going to have a Christmas miracle."

Elizabeth said to Sarah who had been in the shelter helping Lizzie for the past year, "Fetch Joe, we'll need his medical expertise."

"Are you sure Lizzie?" Sarah said. "He is still hung over."

"Put his head in a bucket of water and tell him to get his butt over here because he's needed. I am sure he will be okay," said Elizabeth.

"I hope you are right," said Sarah doubtfully.

Joe, a doctor and alcoholic who hadn't been able to cope with what life had thrown him, ended up on the streets where Elizabeth had found him and brought him to St James's shelter.

Ten minutes later, wet hair slicked back and eyes wide with self-doubt, he was at Mary's side checking her. Elizabeth reassured him that he could do it and all his knowledge would come back to him, as he was really needed to save this young woman and her child.

A few hours later the cry of a new baby brought tears to the eyes of all the people in the shelter. Elizabeth washed the tiny boy, wrapped him and gave him to Mary. "You have brought us our Christmas miracle; here is new life which gives hope to us all."

Mary held her baby son to her heart and looked at all the people who had helped her. Overwhelmed, she couldn't speak. Gabe, Elizabeth, Joe, Sarah and the others in the shelter, smiled at the young mother and her baby and each one was grateful for the blessings brought this Christmas Morning.

A week later when Mary felt stronger she felt she needed to tell someone who knew Jimmy about the birth of his son Matthew. She phoned Kevin and told him her news.

"Thank goodness you called," he said with relief, "I've been trying to track you down. Where are you? I have some news for you too."

They arranged to meet not far from the St James's shelter in a coffee bar. Kevin was there with Pauline, his fiancée. They hugged Mary, admired Matthew, then Mary told them about how her mother had thrown her out; being found by Gabe and taken to the shelter where Matthew was born.

Both young people were distressed at what Mary had to go through alone and apologized for not keeping in touch and being more help.

"I've some good news for you Mary," smiled Kevin. "I couldn't get out of my head that Jimmy would have definitely wanted to care for you and his baby. I contacted his company and talked to his boss, you remember him Mary? We saw him at the firm's leaving dinner for Jimmy."

"Yes I remember, David Parker isn't it?"

"That's right. Now, as Jimmy didn't have any direct family they didn't know who would benefit from the insurance which is taken out on all staff who are going into risky jobs. He agreed that it should go to you and the baby," Kevin said with a huge smile.

Mary was speechless for a moment then gently kissed her sleeping baby on the head. "Your Daddy has looked after you darling, even though I didn't tell him about you, everything is going to be alright."

Kevin arranged a meeting with Mr. Parker and Mary. Mary asked Kevin to come along to help her understand everything. It wasn't an enormous amount of money but enough to take care of them for the next few years and some to be invested for Matthew's education. David Parker was kindness itself and made some suggestions on how she could have a certain amount paid out each month with the rest invested safely.

Within a few weeks of searching for the right place, Mary and Matthew moved into a warm cozy little flat helped by Kevin and Pauline. When she was settled she took Matthew to visit the St James's shelter. She wanted to thank Sister Elizabeth for all the help she and

Matthew had received. Lizzy was delighted to see them and they fussed over Matthew.

A figure stepped forward. It was Joe. He looked different, stronger somehow. He looked at Mary and said, "I have to thank you for having your baby here, you've saved my life."

"And I am sure you saved our lives too Joe, thank you." They smiled at each other.

Joe sat down and told Mary he had contacted the hospital where he had worked and talked everything over with the Chief of Staff. He was checking into a rehab centre, had joined AA and was determined to get his life back on track. Delivering Matthew had shocked him out of his fear that he couldn't cope.

He walked Mary and Matthew back to their little flat and accepted Mary's invitation to stay for something to eat. He walked Matthew up and down while Mary made dinner. Mary told him about Jimmy, and in return he told her about the long hours in A & E. The final straw had been the horrific crash where there were multiple injuries; more than fifty people waiting for treatment, lying on trolleys in the corridors. He had been working for 36 hours when another fatally injured man had died. Joe had fallen into a chair unable to move. A family member of one of the injured had taken a bottle of brandy out of his pocket and handed it to Joe. "Here Doc, you look like you could use a swig."

Joe had taken the bottle, stared at it, then finished it. Then he'd walked out to the nearest pub and drunk until he was thrown out.

Over the next year while Mary cared for Matthew, loving being a mum, Joe was a regular visitor. They supported each other. Joe let Mary catch up on some sleep when sometimes the baby didn't sleep longer than an hour. Mary encouraged Joe when he was depressed and worried if he would manage to complete his papers on pediatrics after he had decided to specialize.

Several years later on Christmas Eve a van turned up at the shelter behind St James's Church. Joe and Mary knocked on the door. Elizabeth gasped in recognition and hugged them both. Turning to the small boy who was with them she said, "Hello Matthew, thank you for coming to visit us at Christmas. Come in, come in."

"We have some Christmas presents for you Lizzie," said Joe and he opened the van. Boxes of food, clothes, blankets, a heater, a radio were all unpacked. Elizabeth and Sarah were stunned.

"How did you know, Joe? We were wondering how we were going to feed everyone, as this has been a very difficult year. Thank you, thank you."

Sitting round the table drinking coffee and eating mince pies from some of the supplies Mary and Joe had brought, they told Elizabeth what had happened since their Christmas miracle.

Joe had been determined to recover and soon after had gone back part-time at the hospital. Not working long, soul-destroying hours but still contributing his skills particularly in the children's ward.

Shortly after Matthew's 2nd birthday Joe asked Mary to move in with him, their relationship had grown into love. They married in the park by the park bench where Mary had met Gabe. Next year Matthew would have a little brother or sister.

Elizabeth ruffled Matthew's hair and said "Did you know the meaning of Matthew's name is Gift from God?"

"He certainly was," said Joe. "Matthew's arrival helped me rebuild my life and I met Mary." He looked with love at Mary and the little boy.

"It's my birthday tomorrow," said Matthew, "and I'm going to be a big brother soon."

"That's wonderful Matthew, you will be a great big brother," replied Lizzie. Everyone remembered the night the baby arrived and how Mary was found by Gabe on the park bench in the snow.

"Have you heard from Gabe, Lizzie?" asked Mary "I owe him so much. If he hadn't turned up at that park bench and I had gone into labour in the snow, neither Matthew nor I would have survived."

"Last time I heard he was in Jerusalem," said Elizabeth. "I never know when he is going to turn up. Miracles always seem to happen when he is around. I wonder sometimes if he is the Angel Gabriel."

Everyone laughed, but a warm feeling in the region of their hearts made each one think secretly Elizabeth might be right.

HOME FROM HOME

(Short Stories for me need to be entertaining and make the reader's imagination take flight. Ernest Hemmingway's classic
"FOR SALE. BABY SHOES. NEVER WORN"
sent shivers of sympathy down my spine and I searched for the story behind the six words. Hope you enjoy sending your imagination soaring with this.

Tommo breathed a sigh of relief as the door closed behind him. He sat on the bed and looked around the small space.

From his bag, he took a picture and an old photograph, both carefully wrapped. He stuck them on the wall at a level he could see when lying down. The picture showed a wild rocky bay with mountains in the distance, hardy sheep grazing and a flock of birds landing on the beach. The photo showed an elderly couple and a small boy. His grandparents were crofters on the Isle of Skye. Tommo had lived with them for several years when 'things were difficult' at home in Glasgow.

A bang on the door, it opened and a friendly voice said,

'Hello Tommo, couldn't cope outside? I wrangled your usual cell for you. I see you've made your 'Home from Home'.

Tommo smiled at the warder and said, 'Thanks, Mr. MacGregor.'

FRIENDS, MEMORIES & A

LEGACY

ERIC found Joe's newly dug grave by a small marker with his name. The Arctic wind insinuated itself through his heavy coat and chilled his bones. He looked up at the dripping winter trees bending in the wind and said, 'Sorry Joe I didn't get here in time to say goodbye. I'll find the others and carry out your wishes. I'll do my best, that's a promise.' He placed a bouquet of winter flowers and foliage on the newly turned soil. Eric nodded and walked out the old graveyard past the ancient church that had stood for centuries in the little village.

It was almost forty years since he had last seen Joe and the others. Growing up they had been such a tight little group. The six children understood each other, didn't judge and had no expectations. In his late teens Eric had immigrated to New Zealand, met Josie a year or so after arriving, they had married and settled in Christchurch. There had been intermittent Christmas cards throughout the years to each other and letters from Marianne; she was good at writing. Somehow life got in the way of them keeping regularly in touch. Until a letter that had been redirected three times dropped into his letter box.

Eric was living in a retirement village. He had retired early when Josie was diagnosed with cancer. She had died a few years ago, and he couldn't face living without her in the home where they had brought up their family. He had two married daughters and four grandchildren. Marie lived in Sydney, Nancy in Auckland, David his son lived in New York. He went on holiday every year to visit them. One year to New York, next Auckland then Sydney. They kept in touch and spoke regularly on Skype, and they visited him in New Zealand when they could.

The battered envelope shocked him, as he recognised the handwriting on the first address; he knew it was Joe. Hands trembling a little he sat down and opened the envelope. A letter dated a month earlier, the address and shaky handwriting told him his old friend was in a hospice not far from where they had all grown up. Joe's old humour came through, he said he was not afraid of meeting *the grim reaper* but he wanted Eric to do something for him. Eric was the youngest of the group and Joe was sure he would still be around.

That evening when he confirmed what time it was in England and checked the phone number of St Mary's Hospice, he called and asked if he could talk with his old friend. A kindly voice told him that Joe had died four days earlier and his funeral had been that day.

Quickly Eric made a decision. He'd go to England, find the others and carry out Joe's request. Full of energy and for the first time in ages, felt he had something outside his normal daily routine that needed doing. Eric got in touch with his children, let them know what he was doing and was pleased they all encouraged him to go ahead and enjoy himself.

'Fly business class Dad,' David said, 'I've got plenty of air points and can organise it for you. Let me know when you want to travel.'

He sat at his computer, pleased he had taken lessons, and looked up white pages in UK. Before long he had found Marianne's phone number. He called thinking if anyone had seen Joe it would be her.

It took a moment or two before she recognised his voice then she sounded delighted to hear from him. She'd been at Joe's funeral with Danny. Over the years with everyone being so busy, somehow they lost track of each other, where they had come from and the only people who knew the real story. Lily and Mick had died some years ago, Mick on holiday in the Caribbean as he had a heart attack when swimming. 'That sounds like Mick, I never thought he would die in bed.' Eric smiled remembering the energetic Mick who had got them into a few scrapes when they were young. He was sorry to hear about Lily, she had been the quietest of the group. He told Marianne he would arrive on Thursday, have a day or so to get over the flight, do a few things and then he would meet them in the pub near the village church, on Saturday, 'If it's still there?' he questioned.

'Oh yes, the Dog and Duck is still going strong, not changed too much,' said Marianne. 'Shall I tell Danny or do you want to surprise him?'

'Let's give him a surprise,' replied Eric smiling, 'as long as it won't give him a heart attack.' Saturday lunch time he'd come into the pub and meet them. Marianne said she'd get Danny organised.

Eric pushed the door of the pub open, grateful for the rush of heat after the pervading chill outside. Shaking his overcoat he hung it up, then looked around the crowded room and saw a woman with a huge smile, wave. He was quickly enveloped in a bear hug from Marianne and when Danny had got over the shock of seeing his old friend again, he shook hands in that very British way, then the men, overcome, hugged each other.

'Before we catch up on the last forty or so years, I have to tell you Joe has a surprise for you – lunch is on him then we are going to revisit our past and maybe it will give us a new lease of life.'

They tucked into the pub's famous beef casserole with dumplings, and after a couple of brandies each they felt warmer and anxious to talk about Joe, Mick, Lily and the connection which bound them when they were small children.

Eric began by telling them about the letter which had been delayed so he was too late to see Joe or attend his funeral. 'His letter was a bolt from the blue and once I had read it a few times I knew I had to carry out Joe's wishes. Yesterday I saw his solicitor; Joe never married, seems he was too busy building his business. Are you ready for this? Eric looked at the two old friends across the table. Joe has left everything to us! His flat in the new complex near the commercial centre in the South of London and a holiday home in Italy. If the solicitor hadn't heard from us within a year it was to be divided up to various charities. We have some big decisions to make. But I suggest that before we do, we visit the solicitor, let him explain how much money is involved then spend a bit of time at the house in Italy. We can decide what would be the best way to carry out Joe's wishes and maybe we can work out the best memorial for him and for us all. What do you think?'

Both Marianne and Danny were widowed like Eric and neither had a partner, so there was no problem in packing up and taking off for Italy. Two weeks later they were relaxing on the beautiful Amalfi Coast in Joe's cool rebuilt farmhouse   overlooking   the   sapphire

Mediterranean. Gina and Sergio who looked after the farmhouse when Joe was away, welcomed them and told them about how Joe had enjoyed coming several times a year to relax. They cooked and looked after Joe's old friends as he had wanted.

The friends had made their decision. Remembering how their early lives were spent they drew up plans for a foundation in Joe's name to care for and educate orphans like themselves and give them opportunities to achieve and make a difference. Arrange mentors, scholarships, opportunities to grow and develop. The house in Italy would be a place for holidays.

A renewed lease of life for the somewhat diminished old gang of young children, all tragically orphaned. Their parents had known each other, were alcoholics or had given up on life. One night they had left the six children they had between them and gone off on a bender. Drunk, they had crawled into an old allotment shed, one of them had dropped a lighted cigarette on an old sack of fertiliser, the shed had gone up and they all had died.

The children were picked up a few days later, starving, dirty and terrified. The village community felt ashamed they hadn't noticed the plight of the children and organised a small orphanage to care for them. They had formed their own little tribe in the orphanage run by the local community and churches. As one of their carers said, 'It's like they have made their own survivors' family, protecting each other and woe betide anyone who upsets them.'

As the sun went down bathing their surroundings in a red and gold light, soft music playing in the background, they raised their glasses to Joe, and their memories. They sat in silence for a little while lost in their own reverie of times past.

Danny said thoughtfully, 'You know I think perhaps we subconsciously didn't keep in touch because only we knew what happened to us before we found the orphanage in the village. As we grew older we didn't want to remember painful memories. We all were a reminder of where we came from.'

They thought for a moment and Marianne said softly, 'you always were a bit of an analytical sod Danny, I think you could be right. We've found each other again, and Joe, Lily and Mike will always be with us. And we'll make great use of the opportunity Joe has given us to ensure he is remembered and please God we can prevent other kids having to experience what we did.

They smiled at each other and knew their lives had purpose and were excited at the project ahead.

THE END

ABOUT THE AUTHOR

Robyn P Murray has enjoyed reading and writing all her life. Growing up in Co. Antrim Northern Ireland, the land of myths and legends, fuelled her passion for storytelling.

After travelling extensively when young she eventually settled in New Zealand and has a son and two grandsons.

In the last few years she has self-published some beautifully illustrated children's books, two anthologies of short stories, and contributed to other books. She enjoys being part of the local writers group, and has read some work on writers on air.